Bad Girl Blues

Bad Girl Blues

by Sally Warner

HarperCollinsPublishers

This is a work of fiction. The characters and events in this story
are not based on real people or events.

Bad Girl Blues
Text copyright © 2001 by Sally Warner

Library of Congress Cataloging-in-Publication Data
Warner, Sally.
Bad girl blues by Sally Warner.
p.   cm.
Sequel to: Totally confidential.
Summary: At the beginning of the sixth grade, twelve-year-old Quinney starts volunteering
at a shelter for stray animals and tackles some tough issues about loyalty and friendship when
her former best friend Marguerite appears to be turning into a "bad girl."
ISBN 0-06-028274-6 — ISBN 0-06-028275-4 (lib. bdg.)
[1. Best friends—Fiction.   2. Friendship—Fiction.   3. Pets—Fiction.   4. Animals—
Treatment—Fiction.]   I. Title.   II. Series.
PZ7.W24644 Bad   2001   00-063171
[Fic]—dc21   CIP
                                                                    AC

Typography by Andrea Simkowski
1   3   5   7   9   10   8   6   4   2

First Edition

To Eli Siems, Will Bosley, and
Julia Bosley, who are never bad.
Well, almost never!

Contents

Bad Girl Blues

CHAPTER ONE
Phone Call

"She dumped me. Marguerite dumped me!" Cree Scovall was almost fourteen, but for a moment he looked a couple of years younger, Quinney couldn't help thinking. She didn't know what to say. Cree leaned way back in the clunky library chair and made a face at her. "Well?" he asked.

"I—I didn't know that," twelve-year-old Quinney said. It was a lie, though, because really, how could any kid *not* know every detail of what was going on with other kids in a town the size of Lake Geneva?

In fact, Quinney Todd had known that Marguerite-and-Cree would be history almost as soon as the thought flitted across Marguerite's brain a week earlier. "I don't want to be tied down when school starts," Marguerite told Quinney as they leaned against the double-trunked birch tree in Quinney's backyard. Marguerite had not gone out with Cree more than a couple of times, and then, only to the bowling alley. But she talked as if they'd been a couple for months. "There are plenty of fish in the sea," she announced as if she'd just invented the saying, "and some of them are in high school."

High school. Trust Marguerite to set her sights on high school before she'd even set foot in middle school. "But I thought you wanted to have a boyfriend when school started," Quinney said. Not that any other sixth graders she knew were dating, or even thinking about it. "I thought that was the whole point." Besides, wasn't Cree the nicest—and *cutest*—boy in town?

"Nope. I don't want Cree—he's all yours, Quin," Marguerite said, laughing. She picked up a handful of leaves and threw them at Quinney.

"I don't want him," Quinney objected, ducking and blushing. "Anyway, Marguerite, it's not like Cree is a bag of popcorn at the movies. You can't just give him away to somebody else when you're done with him."

"Don't take him, then," Marguerite had said, laughing some more. "Let some other girl grab him, if you're feeling so generous."

"Say something," Cree challenged Quinney, landing his chair on the floor with a thunk.

Quinney almost wished she hadn't wandered into the library today. Outside, the September air was like water, cool and clear, and autumn light slanted low through the trees and skipped over the Hudson River like a handful of little flat stones.

Inside, the library was warm, almost stuffy, but three days into the new school year Quinney had wanted to revisit the site of her secret summer job as "professional listener." What a joke, Quinney scolded herself silently. But at least she'd made a little money last summer—and met some interesting people.

Such as Cree—he had been sitting at their old table just when Quinney wandered by, almost as if he'd been waiting for her.

The librarian's gentle voice floated back to the little reference room where Quinney and Cree were sitting. "No," Mrs. Arbuckle was explaining to someone, "you press *Enter* next. . . ."

"I don't *want* to press *Enter* next," a panicky voice objected. "I'm not ready!"

But you couldn't argue with a computer when it was time to press *Enter*, Quinney thought, smiling—any more than you could argue with someone as irrational and stubborn as Marguerite.

"You actually think this is funny?" Cree asked, angry now. "I thought we were friends."

"We are," Quinney said quickly. Sort-of friends, anyway, she corrected herself—because Cree Scovall was in the eighth grade at Adirondack while Quinney was a sixth grader. Cree had been one of Quinney's listening customers over the summer—at least until he found out his professional listener was only a kid. But they'd talked a few times after that. Not often enough to suit Quinney, true, but it was better than nothing.

Officially, they barely even knew each other. Quinney's former summer job was top secret, totally confidential, and both Quinney and Cree intended to keep it that way. Not even Brynnie or Marguerite knew about it, though Quinney had finally told her parents.

"If we're really friends, find out what happened," Cree urged Quinney. "Call her up and ask her, okay?"

Quinney stared down at the scarred library table through her long bangs. "I didn't know you even liked Marguerite all that much. You said it was nothing serious," she finally said, but she spoke so softly that Cree had to lean forward to hear her.

"I *don't* like her that much—especially now," he said, looking surprised at his own words even as he uttered them. "I just want to find out what happened, that's all. There's got to be a logical explanation."

Cree was as big on logical explanations as she was, Quinney thought, hiding another smile. "So why don't you ask her yourself?"

Cree shook his head helplessly and ran his hands back through his shaggy brown hair. "I haven't even seen her around. Not lately."

"Me either," Quinney admitted. She'd barely caught a

glimpse of Marguerite since school began.

"And I called her, but she wouldn't even come to the phone. It would be pathetic to just keep on trying."

Quinney felt a blush creep across her freckled cheeks. It embarrassed her to see Cree act this way—and over Marguerite, who hadn't even deserved all that attention in the first place. Quinney bit her lip at this disloyal thought. Marguerite was supposed to be her friend, after all.

"So will you do it?" Cree was asking.

"I guess," Quinney said reluctantly. "I'll try, anyway, but she'll probably just tell me to mind my own business." That, or something more colorful, Quinney thought.

Quinney walked slowly down Main Street, heading toward home. Since when had life become so complicated? The cozy trio of sworn best friends—Quinney, Marguerite, and quiet little Brynn Mathers—seemed about ready to fly off into the universe, as though flung to the starry winds by— by centrifugal force. Quinney scowled, trying to remember if that was the exact term she wanted.

"Smile!" a woman called out, driving by in an old red Toyota. Quinney's next-door neighbor Mrs. Sansom waved hello through an open window, and Quinney slapped a grin on her face, even though she hated being told to smile.

What if she didn't feel like smiling?

Quinney crossed the street. And there, right next

to the realtors, was a newly papered-over storefront window with a notice that caught Quinney's eye: Whiskertown.

Quinney reached for the phone before she could lose her nerve.

"Hi, Marguerite?"

"Oh, hey, Quinney."

Marguerite sounded funny, as though she'd just been to the dentist. "Are you okay?" Quinney asked.

"Why shouldn't I be okay?"

"Well, I mean, your voice sounds kind of weird, and I didn't see you at school today. I just figured you might be sick or something."

"I'm sick of school, that's all."

"But you shouldn't—"

"Look, don't start telling me what I should and shouldn't do, all right?"

"I wasn't! I only wanted to ask about—"

"Because I know what I'm doing."

"Yeah, right," Quinney snapped. "Cutting school the first week? Sure sounds like you know what you're doing."

"Listen to you. Get a life, Quinney."

"I've got a life."

"If you can call that living."

Quinney took a deep shaky breath. This was worse than she'd imagined, and she hadn't even asked about Cree yet. "Who do you think you are, talking to me like that?"

"Oh, right, when you called to tell me how to live *my* life?"

"I didn't! I only wanted to ask—"

"Next time, just don't. Don't call me, I'll call you. Deal?"

"It's a deal, Marguerite." Quinney slammed down the phone.

CHAPTER TWO

Accident

"Finally, something *new* is happening in boring old Lake Geneva," Quinney announced at dinner that night. "Something exciting." Maybe talking about Whiskertown would make her stop thinking about that infuriating conversation with Marguerite. But what in the world was she going to tell Cree?

The whole Todd family was seated around the kitchen table eating supper: tuna casserole, peas, and cherry tomatoes. Quinney watched five-year-old Mack sneak a handful of cherry tomatoes into his shorts pocket while his twin, Teddy, watched, expressions of alarm and admiration alternating on his round little face.

"You'd think that the first week of a new school would be enough excitement for our Quinney, but no," Mr. Todd observed jovially.

"Middle school isn't as exciting as you might think," Quinney said, spearing a few peas with the tines of her fork. "At least, not the academic part of it."

"I like school," said Teddy.

"School is boring," Mack announced. The boys had just started kindergarten, and Quinney was surprised to hear them disagree. Usually they saw eye-to-eye. "So what new thing is happening?" he added, looking doubtful.

"Yes, what new, exciting thing is happening in our boring old town?" Mrs. Todd asked. She tucked a wayward strand of hair behind her ear.

"Guess," Quinney teased. "I'll give you a hint—it's a new business, and it's on Main Street." Lake Geneva's Main Street had been dotted with boarded-up windows for ages. Although the Adirondack town's economic situation had perked up in the last couple of years, people in town did most of their shopping at big stores in Peters Falls, which was half an hour away. "If you could choose one business you'd like to see right here in our town," she went on, "what would it be?"

"I know what I'd like," Mrs. Todd said immediately. "An art supply store." Mrs. Todd was an artist and part-time preschool teacher, and she had to get most of her art and craft supplies through catalogs. Peters Falls did not have a good art supply store.

"I'd like it to be a used book store," Quinney's father said dreamily. He taught high school in nearby Rocky Creek, but his real passion was Mark Twain—books by him, books *about* him, memorabilia, anything at all along those lines.

"I want it to be a candy store," Teddy said, looking as though he was about to start smacking his lips. "The kind where they make the candy right there in front of your eyes. And maybe they'd ask me to be the taster—do you think?"

"Oh, sure," Mack said sarcastically. "If they don't care when there's nothing left for them to sell. I don't even think there *is* any new business. I think Quinney's making the whole thing up. You liar," he said, turning to his sister.

"Mackster," his mother warned.

"Well, I'm not making it up," Quinney said patiently. "But what about Monty? What would *he* like the new business to be?"

Monty was the twins' imaginary friend. Quinney and her parents joked about him, but the Todd family had learned to take him into account.

"Monty says it's a pet store," Teddy reported matter-of-factly.

Quinney blinked, surprised, then smiled. "Then Monty wins the prize," she said. "He's closest, at least. It's going to be a stray animal shelter, and it's called Whiskertown."

"Hmmph," Mack said, unimpressed. He chewed a little, then asked, "So what's the prize?" Quinney saw him slip a handful of peas into his pocket while Teddy goggled.

"It was just a figure of speech, Mack," his mother said.

"What does that mean?" Teddy asked.

"It means there *is* no prize," Mack said.

"A place called Whiskertown could be a barbershop,

maybe one that wants a cat or dog in it. *Whiskertown*," Quinney's mother said, trying out the name.

"Or maybe it's a place where people can go buy beards," Mack said, starting to get interested.

"And mustaches," Teddy added with enthusiasm.

"How do you know it's an animal shelter, Quinney?" her father asked. "Is there a sign yet?"

"Yes—they put it up today. It says 'Whiskertown' and underneath it says 'Strays welcome.' There was a phone number, too. I wrote it down. Anyway," she continued, "I'm thinking of volunteering there. I'm sure they'll need volunteers."

"Good idea," her father said heartily.

"Norman," her mother said. Then she turned to her daughter. "Quinney, you're only twelve, and you're already volunteering one afternoon a week at the library—that's plenty. School's just begun—there's all that homework, and you need some time to yourself, baby." Mrs. Todd believed in plenty of daydreaming time for her children.

Mrs. Todd was right that Quinney was busy. In fact, in addition to helping Mrs. Arbuckle at the town's small library, Quinney still had one leftover customer from her secret summer job. Charlotte Van Loon. Quinney wasn't going to let her down.

Charlotte was twelve, like Quinney, and had quickly become an almost-friend. Tonight, Quinney could hardly wait for dinner to be over so she could call her. Who needed Marguerite? Wait until Charlotte heard about

Whiskertown, Quinney told herself. This could be the answer to her dog problem!

"Quinney?" her mother asked, interrupting Quinney's rambling thoughts. "Are you even listening to me?"

"Mmm-hmm," Quinney said, nodding. "But I would only work at the animal shelter one afternoon a week," she said. "Two, tops. And they're not giving us that much homework at Adirondack." *And I want to avoid hanging around Marguerite.*

"Can we please be excused?" Teddy asked.

"After you two clear the table," Mr. Todd told the twins. "But quietly, please—and after you finish, your mom and I want to talk to Quinney alone, about something important."

"Ooh, busted," Teddy told his sister sympathetically. He picked up a glass with both hands and carried it to the counter next to the sink, never once taking his eyes from it. Mack gave an exaggerated yawn, indicating his boredom with such domestic chores, but a quick look from his dad inspired him to start clearing, too. He grabbed a handful of dirty silverware, trotted over to the sink, and flung the knives, forks, and spoons over the edge.

"Quietly!" Mr. Todd said, and Quinney had to laugh, even though she wondered what her parents were going to say to her.

Finally, the boys finished and slipped out of the kitchen to watch a video.

"Quinney, was Marguerite in school today?" Mrs. Todd asked as soon as the kitchen door swung shut.

"No," Quinney said.

"Oh, dear, then—it's true," Mrs. Todd said. She went over to a pile of newspapers that sat precariously on the seat of an extra kitchen chair, rummaged for a moment, then handed Quinney the front section.

FIVE HURT IN
LAKE GENEVA ACCIDENT

LAKE GENEVA—Four teenagers and one child were hurt Thursday afternoon in a two-vehicle collision at a local intersection, town police said. The five, all riding in one car, were taken to Peters Falls Hospital. They were treated and released.

The crash occurred at the intersection of River Road and Davis Lane at about 4:15 P.M., when a westbound pickup truck, operated by Roscoe Hurlbut, 42, of Lake Geneva, hit a northbound car driven by Ricky Gernisch, 16, also of Lake Geneva. Apparently the Gernisch car failed to stop at the sign, hitting the Hurlbut truck broadside. Empty beer cans were said to have been found at the scene of the accident.

The driver of the truck was uninjured, but the driver of the car and his four passengers suffered minor injuries, according to the hospital. The passengers were Nick Castleton, 17, Gregory Burnett, 16, Marguerite Harper, 12, of Lake Geneva, and Scott Norell, 17, of Rocky Creek.

Police said no tickets were issued, but the crash is still under investigation.

The Peters Falls Press, Peters Falls, New York

Quinney raised her eyes from the paper, her heart pounding. "What does that mean, 'treated and released'?" she asked her mother. "Is Marguerite okay?" Her friend's voice *had* sounded so strange on the phone, Quinney remembered—thick, and her words were a little slurred. And I thought she'd just gotten up from a nap, Quinney berated herself. I should have known something was wrong!

"The hospital wouldn't have let her go home if there was any question of more serious injury. She probably just took the day off from school to rest," Mrs. Todd said in a reassuring voice. "I called Anita, at work," she added, sounding more concerned, "and at home, but no luck."

"Why didn't you say something sooner?" Quinney asked. Her heart was pounding.

"We were waiting for you to bring it up," Mr. Todd said.

"Weren't all the kids talking about it at school?" Quinney's mother asked.

Quinney shook her head slowly. "No one was. Those guys who were in the accident are all in high school, remember—Marguerite was the only one in middle school. Probably nobody had heard about it yet," she said. "We have to leave for school so early, and you know how they always deliver the paper late to Lake Geneva."

Quinney's father shoved his chair away from the kitchen table and pushed his glasses up high on his nose. "Riding in a car after school with a bunch of beered-up high school boys! I know Scotty Norell, by the way, and he's some piece of work."

"Marguerite probably had a reason for doing what she did," Quinney told him, her voice quavering. But as soon as she said the words, she wished she could take them back. Why was she defending Marguerite? Her friend would have had a reason, all right—but it was sure to be a bad one, judging by the way she'd been acting lately.

Sixth grade, Quinney thought. Sixth grade! You'd think that *idiot* Marguerite could have waited past the first week of middle school to ruin her reputation.

Mrs. Todd shook her head. "This isn't going to do Marguerite any good, there's no way around it. Not in a small town like this."

The kitchen door swung open and Teddy and Mack tumbled into the room. "Ow—quit it," Mack said, rolling himself into a protective ball.

"You quit it," Teddy told him. "You're the one who messed up the video. There's white stripes all over," he informed his dad.

"Well, you can both quit it," Mr. Todd said. "I'll come straighten things out in a minute."

Quinney frowned, trying to concentrate on the problem at hand. Marguerite *deserved* whatever bad things people thought about her if she was going to mess up like this. Maybe it would teach her to be more careful. But who knew what had really happened? Weren't people—even *kids*—supposed to be innocent until proved guilty?

And Marguerite had been her friend for years and years. Perhaps her parents were being unfair. "The beer could have belonged to Mr. Hurlbut—"

The twins giggled. "You said *hurl butt,*" Teddy interrupted.

"Boys," Mrs. Todd said automatically. "Mind your Ps and Qs."

"Mommy said *pee,*" Mack said. Teddy tried to hide his giggles, but little quacks of laughter escaped from behind his hands.

"Okay, that's enough potty talk," Mr. Todd said firmly. "And Mack, what in the world have you got in your pockets?"

Everyone turned to stare at Mack. His bulging pockets made him look a little like a bee, its skinny legs swollen with pollen. "Oh, nothing," he said, sliding his hands into the offending pockets in an attempt to look casual. "I've got nothing in my pockets. Just air."

Mrs. Todd crossed the room in a second to check for herself. "Oh, *ick,*" she exclaimed, pulling out Mack's hand, which was covered with slimy tomatoes and crushed green peas.

"Mack," Mr. Todd said. "To the bathroom, now. March." Mack left, with Teddy following.

"He does that all the time," Quinney said, still furious with her mom and dad for criticizing Marguerite, and at

Mack for interrupting. She brushed angrily at her long bangs.

"You tattletale!" Mack shouted from the other room.

"Shut up!"

"Now, I know we're all upset—especially about Marguerite," Mr. Todd said in the exaggeratedly calm voice of a stressed-out high school teacher, "but Quinney, there's no need for you to snap at your family. That's not going to help the situation."

Nothing was going to help, Quinney thought.

Mrs. Todd walked over to Quinney's chair and kissed the top of her head. "Well," she said, "we can all count our blessings—and hope for Marguerite's sake that this blows over soon. You tell her we're just happy she's okay, when you talk to her."

Right. "Don't call me, I'll call you," Marguerite had said.

"I doubt that I'll be doing that anytime soon," Quinney said, standing up to leave. "But when I do, I'll be sure to give her your message."

Mr. and Mrs. Todd exchanged startled glances as Quinney stalked out of the room.

CHAPTER THREE

Friends

C harlotte Van Loon had several problems, and one of them answered the phone when Quinney called later that night. "Hello?" the cranky voice said.

"Hello, Mrs. Van Loon? It's Mary McQuinn Todd," Quinney said, sinking to the now-dark kitchen's brick-patterned vinyl floor. Mrs. Van Loon insisted upon only recognizing Quinney by her full name. "May I please speak to Charlotte?"

"Didn't you see her just last weekend, Mary McQuinn?" Mrs. Van Loon asked. Quinney could picture her narrow powdery face crease with suspicion. Charlotte went to private school near Lake George, but she and Quinney liked to hang out when they could—which clearly was going to be more difficult now that summer was over.

"Well, yes, but there's something important I need to talk to her about," Quinney said, trying to hide her impatience.

"That girl's accident, I'll bet," Mrs. Van Loon said, and she sniffed. She sounded almost—almost *happy,* Quinney thought, surprised. "Charlotte just got back from walking Harold's dog. Marshmallow," she added, in a voice filled with disgust.

As if Quinney didn't know the name of Charlotte's dog. "Well, can she come to the phone?" Really—this was like trying to get the first pickle out of a jar, Quinney thought.

"I'll get her," Mrs. Van Loon said, sounding reluctant. "But I don't want you asking her to come over to your house tonight, Mary McQuinn. There are some things I need her to help me with at home."

There always were, Quinney thought, sighing, as Mrs. Van Loon went to get Charlotte. She looked around the darkened kitchen and waited.

And waited.

"Hi, Quinney?" Charlotte's voice sounded breathless.

"Hi, Charlotte," Quinney said. The two girls waited until they heard Mrs. Van Loon hang up her receiver. "How's everything going?"

"Not too bad," Charlotte said. But she always said that, no matter what. "Mother is freaking about Marguerite being in that car accident," she added shyly. Charlotte knew that Quinney and Marguerite were friends. "Is she okay?"

"She's fine. Any sign of the puppies yet?" Quinney asked, changing the subject. Marshmallow's belly was huge—the puppies had to come soon.

"No—thank *goodness*," Charlotte said. "Quinney, I'm scared to leave her alone for a minute. You know what my mother says she's going to do."

"I know," Quinney said, grim. Mrs. Van Loon had threatened to have all the puppies destroyed—and Marshmallow, too. Marshmallow was officially her husband's dog, and she was the main thing Mr. and Mrs. Van Loon fought about. When Marshmallow got pregnant, Mrs. Van Loon took it personally. It was the last straw, she had announced.

"I mean, what if the puppies are born when I'm at school?" Charlotte asked. "Mother might just bundle the whole litter up into the car and head for the pound in Peters Falls."

"Well," Quinney said, hoping she was right, "I think I found a solution—Whiskertown."

"Whiskertown? What's that?"

"It's going to be a stray animal shelter, and it's opening up right here in Lake Geneva. They may even want volunteers."

"Oh, it would be so much fun to do something like that," Charlotte said excitedly. "If only my mother would let me."

"We'll work on that later," Quinney said, feeling doubtful about such a thing happening—at least in *this* lifetime. "The important thing is, this could save Marshmallow's life."

"Except that she's not a stray," Charlotte pointed out.

"True," Quinney admitted slowly. "But she *is* an animal who needs shelter. Do you want me to call and ask if Whiskertown can take her?"

"Oh, Quinney, would you?" Charlotte asked.

"Yes, but what's your dad going to say? It's his dog."

"He'll be relieved, I think," Charlotte said, sounding sad.

Privately, Quinney agreed. Mr. Van Loon didn't even seem to *like* Marshmallow anymore. He just liked having something to fight with his wife about. Poor Marshmallow was like a magnet for the Van Loons' quarrels. Quinney wondered what they'd fight about when Marshmallow was gone.

Charlotte, probably.

"Okay—I'll call the Whiskertown person tomorrow," Quinney said. "First I'll volunteer, then I'll ask about Marshmallow."

"Oh, Quinney, thank you," Charlotte said.

There was a click on the line, and Mrs. Van Loon's voice broke into their conversation. "Time to say good night to Mary McQuinn, Charlotte," she said. "Your five minutes are up."

"And she had the nerve to call *me* trash," Brynn Mathers said the next morning. She and Quinney were stretched out on the chipped green picnic tables next to the lake, enjoying the unexpectedly warm weather.

"Marguerite?" Quinney asked.

"Of course, Marguerite—who else do we talk about?"

Quinney scowled, squinting up at the sun. "But why on earth would she say something like that to you? It doesn't even make sense."

"Oh, she was really mad when she said it—because I told her that she was wearing too much makeup. So she called me trashy, just because I happen to live in a mobile home. As if me and my mom had a choice. But *she's* the one who's been acting trashy, and now the whole world knows it." Brynn sat up and hooked her wispy blond hair behind her ears. There was a fierce expression on her face, but Quinney could see a line of tears ready to fall from her friend's lower lashes.

Calling Brynnie trash . . . no wonder Brynn was upset. That was pretty harsh—and Brynn was the last person you'd say that about, in Quinney's opinion. Brynn was always as sparkling as a brand-new Christmas doll, and her mom made sure that her clothes were clean and ironed. Mrs. Mathers even ironed Brynnie's *socks*, for Pete's sake.

Sighing, Quinney gazed up at the gaudy autumn trees and bushes that surrounded the two girls in the little lake-side park. The leaves would soon fall, she knew. Red maple, soft maple, sumac, ash; autumn came early to this part of upstate New York.

"You don't even care," Brynn said, disgusted. She flopped back down.

"Yes, I do," Quinney said. "But what do you want me to say?"

"That she's wrong!" Brynn exploded.

"Well, of course she's wrong."

"So say it. Anyway, it's not like I didn't try to warn her," Brynn said.

"You warned her?" Quinney asked.

"I just thought Marguerite should know what kids were saying, that's all," said Brynnie. "So I called her on Wednesday night and told her how everyone in Adirondack Middle School was gossiping that here she was, a sixth grader, hanging out at the high school. It was for her own good," she added, lifting her small round chin in the air.

"What did Marguerite say?"

"Well, she swore up and down that it was no big deal. 'No biggie,' you know," Brynn reported. "She told me that she wouldn't do anything you or I wouldn't do."

"Huh," Quinney said. "And what was *that* supposed to mean?"

"I guess it meant that she wasn't doing a single, solitary thing," Brynn said, laughing a little, "because I'm sure not, and I don't think you are either. But it was a big fat lie, obviously. And now she's paying for it."

"I guess," Quinney said, put off by Brynnie's enthusiasm.

"You *guess?*"

Quinney tried to sound reasonable. "We don't know the whole story about what happened. Maybe it was just— just an innocent car accident."

"Thank goodness we *don't* know the whole story," Brynn retorted. "Well, if you want to believe her, that's *your* problem." She sniffed. "Marguerite keeps saying she wants to get out of Lake Geneva some day, but you watch—she'll be pregnant before she knows it. And then everything will be over for her. I mean, I hope I'm wrong, and everything . . ."

"I hope so too," Quinney said, shocked by the turn this conversation had taken.

"I just hate her!" Brynn blurted out. "She was wrong to call me trash."

It was strange, Quinney realized guiltily—she had no idea things had gotten this bad between Brynn and Marguerite. Marguerite had taken up so much time and attention over the last part of the summer that poor Brynnie just about disappeared off Quinney's radar screen. *It's like the craziest friend sucks up all the energy*, Quinney thought.

"Tell the truth," she said suddenly, challenging her friend—because Brynnie *didn't* hate Marguerite, she was pretty sure, any more than Quinney did.

It was an old game the girls had played since they were eight: If you were ordered to tell the truth, you had to say the first thing that popped into your head, no matter how weird it sounded.

"Okay," Brynnie said reluctantly. "I—I guess I'm a little bit afraid of Marguerite, but I don't know why. Your turn."

"Well," Quinney said. "I hate to say it, but I think my family grew better tomatoes this summer than you guys did."

Both girls laughed, relieved. The tension was broken.

"Want to come home for lunch?" Quinney asked, sitting up. "Mom's making cookies."

"With the twins?" Brynn asked, looking doubtful. As an only child, the twins made her nervous—though Teddy and Mack adored her.

"Yes. But they'll leave us alone if I tell them to," Quinney said, coaxing.

She hoped Brynn would come. There had been an empty feeling in her chest ever since she'd heard about the accident, and she did not want to be alone. Marguerite obviously wouldn't be coming over; she was still holed up at home, not speaking to Quinney. And Mrs. Van Loon kept Charlotte as busy as a marine doing chores on Saturday mornings.

I'm running out of friends, she thought gloomily.

"Let's go," Brynnie said, jumping to the ground. "My stomach is growling so loud, I can barely hear myself think."

CHAPTER FOUR

Spot

After a quick Saturday lunch of grilled cheese sandwiches, which the twins ate sneaking starry-eyed glances at Brynn, Quinney and Brynn climbed the stairs to Quinney's room. Three faded rag rugs warmed the room's honey-colored wood floor. One of Mrs. Todd's landscape paintings—horses crossing the Hudson, with soft round hills cloaked in autumn colors—glowed between the room's two windows, their white ball-fringed curtains flung wide to let in the light. Peach-colored walls seemed to provide a glow of their own. Quinney flopped down on her bed and looked at the phone number she had copied from the sign on the Whiskertown storefront. Brynn curled up on the other bed with a pile of old magazines.

WHISKERTOWN, the sign had read. *Opening soon. For more information, call 2990.* All Lake Geneva phone numbers had the same first three numerals, so when you gave out a phone number, you only had to give the last four digits. That made the numbers a lot easier to remember.

Quinney went to make the call from the phone at the end of the hallway. "Yes, hello? Edith Mudge here," a brisk voice answered. Quinney heard a puppy yip in the background.

"Hi—this is Quinney Todd. I'm calling about Whiskertown." Quinney was nervous.

"What about it?" the woman asked, sounding suspicious.

"Well, um, I live here in town, and I was just wondering if—if you need any volunteers?"

"I *am* looking for volunteers," Edith Mudge said. "But not just anyone. Tell me about yourself."

"Well, Miss Mudge," Quinney said, noticing that the name came out sounding like *Miss Smudge*—"I'm twelve, and like I said, I live right here in Lake Geneva. And I have some work experience."

"Such as?" the woman inquired sternly.

"Right now I'm volunteering at the library one afternoon a week." Quinney decided not to mention her listening business. A no-nonsense-sounding person like Miss Mudge wouldn't be too impressed by something like *that*, she thought.

"The library. Hah," Miss Mudge said, sounding scornful. "No animals there—they aren't allowed. Tell me about your pets."

Oh, no, Quinney thought. "We—we don't have any," she admitted.

"Why on earth not?" Miss Mudge asked, much shocked.

"Well, it's my dad. We used to have this dog named Spot, but he died when I was only two."

"What kind?"

"Excuse me?"

"What kind of *dog*?" Miss Mudge asked impatiently.

"Oh. He was a black Labrador."

"Solid black, no spots. So why did your parents call him Spot?"

"They thought it was funny, I guess," Quinney said, embarrassed. Her parents' sense of humor hadn't changed much over the years. "They got him before I was born," she added, to make it clear the name hadn't been her idea.

"So what happened to him?"

"This guy working on our house accidentally let him out when my mom and dad weren't home, and then the dog got run over, and my dad told my mom, 'No more pets, period.'" Quinney had asked for one, many times, but Mr. Todd had never changed his mind.

"Hmmph," Miss Mudge said, mulling this over. "And just what do you think you have to offer *me*? I need someone who has experience with animals."

"Well," Quinney said, trying fast to think of something. "I'm a good worker, and I learn quickly. Also, I'm good around people." Yeah, right, she found herself thinking—if she was so good around people, then how come one of her very best friends didn't even call her when she was in a car accident?

"You're good with *people*?" Miss Mudge asked, as impressed as if Quinney had confided that she could fly. "You can talk to them and everything? *Politely*?"

"Sure," Quinney said, surprised. "And I listen, too."

"Well, that's more than I can do," Miss Mudge admitted flatly. "I seem to rub everyone's fur the wrong way. Don't know why. Of course, I've never met a person yet who could measure up to your average house pet."

"Oh," Quinney said. She'd never heard anyone talk this way, but she decided to follow up on the one thing that had impressed Miss Mudge. "You're going to need someone in Whiskertown who is good around people. This is a small place, and if you get off on the wrong foot with the folks here, they won't let you forget about it for years."

"You're probably right," Miss Mudge said. "Some of the idiots who came into my last shop—well, you should have heard the fool things they said."

"Where was that, Miss Mudge?"

"Over in Vermont. Town got built up, though. Pricey, and crowded to boot. I decided we all needed a change. Me, my animals—well, that whole Vermont town needed a change, as a matter of fact. So I obliged them and left." She paused, as if waiting.

By the time Quinney realized Miss Mudge had made a sort of joke, it was too late to laugh. So, instead, Quinney said, "Well, maybe I can help out with the people. I know Lake Geneva pretty well."

"That's a plus. And if you're a hard worker and willing to learn, then I'm willing to take a chance on you. Can you start tomorrow?"

"Tomorrow? Sunday? But you aren't even open yet."

"You're arguing with me *already*? I told you, you can help out. Yes or no?"

"Okay—yes," Quinney said. "I have to help my mom prepare some stuff for her nursery school class, but I can come in after ten-thirty."

"It's settled, then. You know where the place is?"

"Yes. Uh, Miss Mudge, can I ask you something else?" Quinney said, remembering her promise to Charlotte.

"If it's quick. Got to brush Senator."

"Well, it's about a dog," Quinney said, trying not to stumble over her words. "She's about to have puppies, and the woman whose husband owns her says that's the last straw, and she's going to have them all destroyed— Marshmallow, too. That's the mother."

"What's wrong with her?"

"With Marshmallow? Nothing. I guess she chews her tail a little, but—"

"Not the dog! Of *course* the dog chews her tail—she's a nervous wreck, probably. Wouldn't you be, if you lived with someone who hated your very whiskers? No, I meant what's wrong with the woman?"

"Oh." That was a good question, Quinney thought—what *was* wrong with Mrs. Van Loon? "I'm not really sure. I think she just likes to fight with her husband about Marshmallow. Maybe this would be her way of finally winning the battle."

"Dis-gusting," Miss Mudge announced. "Of *course* we'll help poor Marshmallow. Get her spayed, too, after she whelps. Find good homes for her litter. Bring her on over," she said, as if she had just invited the dog to a last-minute dinner party.

"Oh, thanks, Miss Mudge. I'll—I'll talk to her owner tomorrow."

"And I'll see you at ten-thirty," Miss Mudge said, "Quinney, was it? Oops—Senator is waiting. Got to go."

And with that, she hung up.

CHAPTER FIVE

No Logical Connection

It was Sunday morning, and Quinney still hadn't heard from Marguerite.

Not a word. And Quinney absolutely refused to be the one to call first.

Well, there were plenty of other things to think about.

The breakfast dishes were done, and Mr. Todd and the boys had gone out to throw rocks in the river. Quinney was in the dining room, which was now her mother's studio, and was sitting at the old dining table. "Mom," she asked as they cut out big orange pumpkin shapes from construction paper, "how come Dad never let us get another pet after Spot died?"

Mrs. Todd paused in her work. "Another pet?" she asked, frowning. "What are you up to, Quinney?"

"Nothing, I swear. Wow, talk about suspicious," Quinney said, a little irked. "I'm just curious, that's all. I mean, it seems kind of strange. Most families have *something*, even if it's only a hamster. But Dad always said no."

"Quinney, that's not quite fair. You haven't asked for a pet in years, and the twins don't seem especially interested in animals yet."

"I haven't asked in years because I always knew what the answer would be if I did," Quinney pointed out. "Remember? I asked for a puppy once, and for a kitten from that litter Marguerite's cat had. And I begged and begged about that bunny from my second-grade class."

"I remember him," her mother said. "AnyBunny. What a sweet little creature he was."

"So how come you wouldn't let me adopt him?"

"Quinney, your father—oh, it's too hard to explain."

"I still think we could have had some kind of a pet. Other families do it." Quinney didn't believe that her mother couldn't explain if she tried. But all she said was, "The twins and I would help out. And Monty, too," she added, trying to lighten the atmosphere.

Her mother thought for a moment. "It's a lot of work, having a pet. And it can be expensive."

"You're talking about having another baby, and that's work and money—more than a pet, I bet," Quinney said.

"I'm not pregnant yet," Mrs. Todd observed sadly.

"Well, it could happen." Quinney tried not to think about it too often, though.

"With any luck," Mrs. Todd answered.

They cut a few more pumpkin shapes out of the construction paper.

"What was it like when you guys had a dog?" Quinney asked.

Mrs. Todd sighed and stopped working. She stared at her small square hands. "I remember that when we got Spotty, your father and I just fell head over heels in love with him. We didn't have you children then, you know—Spot was kind of like our baby. Then you came along, Quinney, and, of course, we fell in love with *you*."

"What about Spot? Was he jealous of me?"

"Oh, a little, maybe, but pretty soon he was just as crazy about you as we were." Mrs. Todd smiled, remembering, and she put down her scissors. "That dog used to sit next to your playpen and guard you, then he'd bark for me to come when you'd wake up."

"He did?" Quinney was delighted.

"Sure—and he'd let you climb all over him. 'Spotty Mountain,' we used to call him."

"Then why—"

"I think that when Spot was run over, your father got—well, *scared*, somehow. I know it doesn't make any sense, but I think he realized for the first time that it was possible something bad could happen to you, too."

"But that's crazy. There's no connection," Quinney objected.

"Of course not," her mother admitted. "No logical

connection at all. But, Quinney, you don't know how help-less you can feel when you're a new parent. Maybe Spotty's death made your dad feel even *more* helpless, and he just couldn't stand it."

"I never got run over," Quinney said stubbornly.

"Well, no," her mother said. "But I think the idea of being responsible for one more life—even if it were a kitten's life, or a bunny's—was simply too much for him to contemplate. I don't know that for sure, though, Quinney—we never really talked about it. It's just a hunch."

And her mother's hunches were usually pretty good, Quinney thought. "But you think he might be over that feel-ing now?" she asked her mother. After all, he'd gotten over it enough for them to have the twins, and now maybe-baby.

"He might be," her mother answered, but her voice was doubtful. "It's hard to say. Still, I think your father is entitled to be at least a little weird about this one thing, don't you? When he's so normal in every other way?"

Yeah, right, Quinney thought, hiding a smile.

CHAPTER SIX

Charlotte

It was still only nine forty-five when Quinney and her mom finished preparing the craft project, so Quinney decided to walk over to Charlotte's house before going to Whiskertown. She didn't call Charlotte first; she was afraid that Mrs. Van Loon might answer the phone.

The Van Loons had moved to Lake Geneva early in the summer. Charlotte was an only child, which Quinney sometimes secretly longed to be. But Quinney didn't envy Charlotte. Her parents were awful. Mrs. Van Loon was the worst, suspicious and overly strict, but Mr. Van Loon wasn't much better. He let his wife push him around, resisting her bossiness only in small, feeble ways. For instance, one time, Quinney saw him sweep out the garage as ordered, but then he pushed the pile of the debris behind a folded-up card table rather than pick it up.

Mr. Van Loon was so quiet and meek that sometimes Quinney wanted to yell *boo!* at him. She just hoped he would have the nerve to help them save poor Marshmallow.

If you were an only child with awful parents, Quinney thought, everything must seem more—more *more*, in a way. Like frozen lemonade concentrate, undiluted; their undivided attention would be inescapable.

But Quinney had to admit that sometimes Charlotte herself could be aggravating, too.

There was that time she spent the morning complaining to Quinney about how her mom made her keep everything in her bedroom *just so*, like in a magazine photograph, but when Quinney accidentally knocked a stack of old *Seventeen* magazines to the floor, Charlotte instantly made Quinney pick them up and stack them neatly, with all the edges lined up. And her mother hadn't been anywhere around, then.

And there was the time at the end of the summer when Charlotte had begged to go bowling with Quinney, Marguerite, and Brynn. But at Bowl-A-Lot, Charlotte complained about the shoes and the popcorn and how much nicer the bowling lanes were in her old town. Then, the next day, she'd had a few choice words to say about Brynnie and Marguerite.

"Brynn keeps fiddling with her hair, and she lets

Marguerite do all the talking. And then Marguerite never shuts up, does she?"

It was sad, really.

Quinney never told Brynn or Marguerite what Charlotte said about them, but even so, neither girl wanted to be around Charlotte again. "She gives me the creeps," Marguerite announced after that one meeting. "Besides, she looks funny."

"That's probably because her mother chooses her clothes most of the time," Quinney said, thinking of Charlotte's matching shorts sets, perky lace-trimmed pastel sundresses, and the white sandals Mrs. Van Loon made her polish every night. Charlotte always had tiny white crescents of shoe polish under her fingernails.

Even Brynnie, usually so easygoing and tolerant, said, "I don't know, Quinney—she's okay, I guess, but it was hard having fun with her around. It's like you can't *relax*. You're just waiting for her to criticize something."

Still, Quinney thought, walking down the long shady drive to the Van Loons' riverside home, I like Charlotte—in small doses, anyway. When the two of them were alone together, Charlotte could be so funny! She could imitate anyone—her own mother, even herself. And she was great with the twins. She always entered into their games right away.

Charlotte was sweeping the front porch as Quinney neared the Van Loons' big old house. She was wearing crisp khaki pants, Quinney noticed, and the white sandals, and a white shirt with a round Peter Pan collar buttoned clear up to her neck. And she was wearing an apron. She waved at Quinney.

Mrs. Van Loon had decorated the front lawn with two painted cement deer, and a huge plastic butterfly was attached to the side of the house. Maybe she just didn't like *real* animals, Quinney thought, waving back.

"Hi," Quinney said, when they were close enough to talk without shouting.

"Hi." Charlotte was quiet, subdued today.

"Is your dad home? Because I'm supposed to talk to him about Marshmallow," Quinney said, stepping onto the porch.

"No, he went in to the office."

"On a Sunday?"

"He says fall is a busy time for him," Charlotte replied. "Why? Did you talk to the Whiskertown person?"

"Yes, and she said she'd take Marshmallow *and* find homes for the puppies."

"Oh, Quinney!" Charlotte was thrilled; her expression brightened.

"But we have to get permission from the official owner," Quinney warned her. "That's why I need to talk to your dad."

Charlotte's face resumed its worried look. "My mother will hear if you call him from the house."

Quinney thought for a moment. "Maybe I can call from

Whiskertown, if you give me his work number."

Charlotte nodded eagerly.

"Now," Quinney continued, "here's what *you're* going to have to do, Charlotte."

"Me?" Charlotte squeaked.

"You," Quinney repeated firmly. "So listen carefully. . . ."

CHAPTER SEVEN

Whiskertown

Quinney knocked timidly at the Whiskertown door, not knowing what to expect. The inside of the display windows on either side of the door had been papered over, hiding all the work that was going on inside. She heard muffled country music and the sound of someone warbling along with it.

Quinney knocked again, harder, and the door swung open. "Quinney—Todd, is it?" a voice asked.

Quinney stared up—*way* up—at the woman who had answered the door, then she put out her hand. "Miss Mudge? How do you do?"

Miss Edith Mudge was almost six feet tall—that was the first thing you noticed about her. She was also very skinny. Her black hair was scraped up into a bun she wore high on her head. What looked like two shiny red chopsticks were jabbed through the bun, and so was a pencil. She looked a little like the Statue of Liberty, Quinney thought, hiding a smile.

Miss Mudge wore a long crinkled skirt, a plain white T-shirt with cat hair all over it, and brown sandals. Dangly beaded earrings hung from her earlobes.

Miss Mudge took Quinney's hand and hauled her into the shop, shutting the door behind them. There was a strong antiseptic pine scent in the air; obviously, Miss Mudge liked to keep things sanitary at Whiskertown.

The shelter's main room wasn't any bigger than her living room at home, Quinney saw. Its walls were lined with three big airy cages, and several binlike enclosures marched down its middle. There was a small fenced-off area toward the rear of the store that seemed to be a snoozing area—for cats, at the moment—and to Quinney's right, a freshly painted red desk glowed like a lighthouse. Papers drifted in untidy piles over its surface, although several large rocks were plunked here and there, holding things down. Pretty primitive, Quinney thought, itching to straighten things up. She was famous for her own organization skills.

"You make Martha Stewart look like an absolute flake," Marguerite had told her once, watching her fold laundry.

On the floor next to the desk, a battered radio was turned up loud. Several cats surrounded it, appearing to listen intently. "I'm countrified—I like my chicken fried!" Quinney heard a man's voice sing, and the cats seemed to nod in agreement.

"Don't want Senator to get out. Doesn't know the

neighborhood yet," Miss Mudge said, gesturing toward the front door. A dignified striped tiger cat butted his big head against Quinney as the woman spoke, and Quinney leaned down to pet him. Large and dusty, he obviously belonged to Miss Mudge. He started to purr.

The tall woman tilted her head down to look Quinney over, and a chopstick fell onto the floor. "*Todd*, it suits you," she said at last. "Name has to do with foxes—red hair and all. It's Saxon, you know—either that, or old Scots. They spelled it with one *D*, though."

"Well, we spell it with two *D*s, and my hair's really more of a brown," Quinney said firmly. She hated the idea of having red hair—she'd been teased about it a hundred times too often to be a good sport.

Miss Mudge considered Quinney's words. "No, it's red," she decided. "Like an Irish setter. But I hope you're smarter. Not that they aren't a perfectly nice breed."

"It's probably just the light in here," Quinney insisted. "My hair is really more of a brown. Well, maybe a browny red."

"Stubborn, too," Miss Mudge said, satisfied. "*Just* like an Irish setter. But enough chitchat. Here's what needs doing first. . . ."

The large, square, plywood enclosures on the floor were going to serve as temporary housing for animals awaiting adoption. The enclosures were open at the top and tall enough to keep small children from touching the animals inside. Quinney could just picture a happy Marshmallow and her squirming litter nestled in one of them.

Quinney was set to work sanding the insides of the enclosures smooth. No animal setting its paw in Whiskertown would ever get a splinter, not if Miss Mudge had anything to say about it! Senator watched Quinney carefully from nearby. He continued to purr loudly through his nose the whole time.

"Don't sand the outsides," Miss Mudge told Quinney. "If some human being comes in here who is careless enough to pick up a splinter, we certainly don't want him picking up one of our animals," she said—somewhat illogically, Quinney thought.

Quinney liked Miss Mudge's use of the word *we*, though; she already felt as though she was part of things at the shop.

The work was fun, too. The troubling thoughts that bounced around in her head like popcorn kernels spilling out of a movie theater popper seemed to disappear as she sanded.

Cree? She'd figure out what to say to him about Marguerite when the time came.

Charlotte? Things would be better for her once Marshmallow was safe.

And Marguerite? So she hadn't called yet—so what?

By the time Quinney got up enough nerve to ask if she could use the phone to call Mr. Van Loon at work, she and

Miss Mudge were comfortable with each other, although all Miss Mudge had said was, "Good, Quinney," as Quinney finished sanding each enclosure. Her new boss thought of her as a sort of dog, loyal, and useful to have around, Quinney realized, punching the Peters Falls office number Charlotte had given her. The thought didn't bother her. Actually, it was kind of nice.

Mr. Van Loon sounded nervous but determined, once Quinney explained the situation to him. "I'll be there in an hour to sign the form," he said.

"Thank you, Mr. Van Loon," Quinney told him. "I know it's the right thing to do."

"Me, too," he said. "I—I sure will miss her, though. She's been a very sweet little doggy."

Miss Mudge snorted when Quinney told her what Mr. Van Loon had said. The two of them were taking a break; Miss Mudge sat in a chair with her feet propped up on her desk, and Quinney sat cross-legged on the wood floor, a loudly purring Senator lolling across her lap.

"'Very sweet,' he calls her, but then he lets his wife treat her that way. That's what's wrong with marriage, Quinney—someone's got to be alpha dog, and then the other partner turns into mush. And it's obvious who's mush in *that* relationship. 'Sweet,'" Miss Mudge repeated scornfully. "Why didn't he just buy a candy bar if he wanted sweet?"

"But at least he's trying to help Marshmallow now.

And I don't think marriage is always like that," Quinney objected, thinking of her own parents. She scratched behind Senator's ears. "It does seem that way with the Van Loons, though," she added hurriedly, seeing the look on Miss Mudge's face. She'd better not forget who was alpha dog here, Quinney reminded herself. "Anyway," she continued, changing the subject, "Mr. Van Loon says he'll stop by in less than an hour to sign the release form."

"I can hardly wait," Miss Mudge said dryly.

A soft knock sounded at the door, and Quinney rose to answer it, leaving a now-grouchy Senator sprawled on the floor. It was Charlotte—and Marshmallow, who sat swollen on the doorstep, panting and blinking in the noontime sun. Charlotte glanced over her shoulder as if nervous that her mother might come chugging after them. "Come on in," Quinney said.

Miss Mudge quickly shut the door behind them. She ignored Charlotte but hurried over to Marshmallow and sank to her knees next to the swaying dog. She fluttered her fingertips over the animal's chest and legs, then gently felt her swollen belly. "Soon," she announced. "Very soon."

"Charlotte, this is Miss Mudge," Quinney said, introducing them. "She owns Whiskertown. And that's Senator over there," she added, gesturing toward the cat. Senator had jumped onto Miss Mudge's desk and was glaring at Marshmallow.

Marshmallow started to chew her tail.

"How do you do," Charlotte said politely. "Thank you for rescuing Marshmallow, Miss Mudge."

"No problem, my dear," Miss Mudge said, surprisingly mild. "No fault of yours—in fact, you've *saved* the dog."

Relieved, Charlotte turned to Quinney. "I sneaked out with the dog, but I better get back home, or my mother will get suspicious." She knelt down and stroked Marshmallow's floppy ears. "Good-bye, doggy," she said, looking as if she was about to start crying. Marshmallow looked up at Charlotte with pleading eyes.

"Now, now," Miss Mudge said, her voice brisk. "It's not good-bye, you two—you'll see each other again."

But it would never be the same for them, Quinney thought. Once big things changed, like—like losing a friend, maybe, or having a new baby come into the house, there was no way things could ever stay the same.

"Perhaps you can come by here and help out from time to time, Charlotte," Miss Mudge was saying.

"Oh, do you think I could?" Charlotte asked, her eyes bright with excitement. Then her expression changed to worry. "But what about Mother? After she finds out Marshmallow is gone, I don't know *what* will happen."

"Bring your mother over and I'll explain the situation to her," Miss Mudge said. "In fact," she added grimly, "I'm quite looking forward to it."

Oh-oh, Quinney thought. Miss Mudge meeting Mrs. Van Loon—it would be the clash of the Titans!

CHAPTER EIGHT
Adirondack Middle School

Adirondack Middle School was one of the newer buildings in Lake Geneva. Outside, its low-slung design—enlivened by golden bricks and sparkling windows—seemed to promise an orderly educational experience. However, the school's crowded hallways sounded with such chaotic noise before the first bell rang that it seemed impossible for a thought to stay in anyone's head.

On this gray Monday morning, it was as though the entire school was ready to pole-vault right over the school week and straight into the following weekend.

"Jeez," Quinney said, cringing against her locker. Several eighth-grade boys thundered past, huge T-shirts billowing behind them like spinnakers. Thank goodness Cree wasn't among them, Quinney thought.

Eighth graders seemed twice as big as the sixth-grade kids did, and most of them were three times as loud. Seventh graders were only twice as loud.

One boy's baseball cap fell off, and he yelped out an angry curse. His friends hooted and jeered at him. "Loser!" one of them cried.

"Hey, Quinney," Brynn shouted, two lockers down.

"What?" Quinney asked, cupping her hand to her ear.

"I said, *'Hey,'*" and the two girls laughed a little. Brynn fiddled with a wisp of long blond hair and shook her head.

"This is the one thing I didn't expect about middle school," Quinney called out.

"What is?" Brynn shouted back.

"The noise," Quinney said, slamming her dented locker door shut as if for emphasis.

She could only imagine what high school would be like.

Brynn twirled the dial of her own lock, then tested the smudged metal door to make sure the lock had really worked. "We'd better go or we're going to be late," she said.

They lowered their heads and began working their way down the crowded hall. They climbed a flight of stairs, Quinney in front. The two girls stayed well to the right of the stairwell so that they wouldn't get trampled by kids barreling down in the opposite direction.

Quinney found herself hoping that no one at school had heard over the weekend about Marguerite's accident. Hah—*right.*

Would Marguerite even come to school today?

Quinney and Brynn slipped into their first-period language arts class just in time to hear Erika Koopman say, "I'll bet she doesn't even have the nerve to show up." Erika was always at the center of things—through sheer word power, Quinney sometimes thought, for the girl certainly always had something to say, someone to put down, somebody to ridicule. Erika tugged at the hem of her snug pink T-shirt with both hands, safe in the knowledge that Mr. Laurence was still outside leaning against the side of the building, where he thought no one could see him taking a few last puffs from his cigarette. She looked around with satisfaction and smoothed back her springy black hair.

Quinney sneaked a look at her. Erika was almost as well developed as Marguerite, Quinney mused, glancing down at her own nearly flat chest. And that was the weird thing about sixth graders—the physical differences among them. It was embarrassing.

Well, at least Brynnie wasn't sticking out all over the place either, yet.

"I wouldn't ever come back to school if I were her," another girl said. "Going for a ride after school with four high school guys!"

"She wasn't even *in* school on Thursday afternoon when it happened," Erika informed everyone. "She cut— and it was just the first week! She's *bad.*"

Quinney and Brynn exchanged a brief look as Mr. Laurence slipped into the room. Brynn's tight little smile said *"I told you so,"* and Quinney looked away. For that one second, she hated Brynn.

Mr. Laurence busied himself at his desk for a moment. Erika spotted Quinney. "Hey, you guys are friends," she said in her most piercing whisper, an avid look spreading across her face. "What happened? Were you there too?"

Heads turned in Quinney's direction, and Quinney felt her face get hot.

"We already know what happened," another girl announced gleefully. "She was on her way to the river with the worst boys in high school, and they were drinking, that's what happened."

She. They didn't even have to say Marguerite's name, and everyone knew who they were talking about.

So Marguerite was finally famous. That had always been one of her main goals in life, Quinney thought sourly. She'd said so often enough, only she probably hadn't meant that she wanted to be famous for something as stupid as *this*.

Well, it served her right.

"Quinney barely knows Marguerite," Brynn piped up.

"Liar," Erika said, not even looking at her. First-period bell jangled, and the kids jammed their backpacks under their seats.

Quinney scowled. She could almost feel her friend trying to catch her eye as their teacher quickly took attendance, but she wouldn't look at Brynn. She had gone too far—publicly denying that Quinney and Marguerite were friends. Not that Quinney felt much like bragging about it herself, at this point.

But how would Brynnie like being abandoned in a time of need?

"Quinney Todd? Ms. Mary McQuinn Todd?" Mr. Laurence asked with exaggerated patience, interrupting her troubled thoughts. A few dutiful kids in the front rows laughed.

"Oh—here," Quinney said, blushing.

He could see that she was here, couldn't he? Why did teachers *do* that?

Mr. Laurence shook his head, pretending to be disappointed in her. "Attention wandering already, Ms. Todd? So early?" he asked, taking an exaggerated look at his Mickey Mouse watch, which he probably wore in an attempt to appear sort of sixties-cool.

Pitiful.

The dutiful kids laughed again, looking back at Quinney. Quinney gave one of them—a washed-out girl named Carla—a fierce look.

Surprised, Carla blinked her eyes once, shrank back in her chair, and started going through her notebook as if she were looking for something so important that it couldn't wait another second.

Huh, Quinney thought.

Mr. Laurence's voice droned endlessly, but Quinney

was too distracted even to try and listen. Instead, she pretended to take notes in her spiral binder; the inky blue circles her ballpoint pen was making must have looked like writing from where Mr. Laurence was standing.

Loop, loop, loop. Why should she feel bad about not defending Marguerite better? Marguerite was making her old friends look like fools.

Loop, loop, loop. But Marguerite was the fool! She could be dead now, just for the sake of riding in a car with Scotty, or Scooty, or Snotty, or whatever his name was.

Loop, loop, loop. And why hadn't Marguerite called over the weekend? She'd had three whole days to pick up the phone. A friend should tell a friend when that friend had been in a car accident. A friend shouldn't have to read about a friend's accident in the newspaper.

Loop, loop, loop.

"Shove over," a heavy blond guy said at lunch, throwing himself into a green plastic chair. He jabbed his chapped freckled elbow in Quinney's direction, and she quickly scootched her chair away from his.

Quinney took a self-conscious bite of her cafeteria taco, and a drop of orange oil splatted onto her tray. She put her napkin on the spot of grease and looked around the crowded room. She wished she had someone to eat lunch with, but Brynn had been assigned second lunch period, and—it being only the second week of school—

Quinney had yet to settle into a comfortable routine.

There had been no sign of Marguerite all morning.

Quinney moved a little farther away from the boy, who was sprawling in that confident way some boys had.

Another boy sat down across from her, flinging his long, skinny leg over his chair as if he were climbing onto a horse. He was in the seventh grade, Quinney thought, but she didn't know his name. She put down her taco, pretending that she was through eating, and dabbed self-consciously at her fingers with the soiled napkin. She stood up.

"Hey," the first boy said. "We didn't say you could leave."

"Yeah—sit down," the second boy said, grinning at her.

Quinney wanted to go, but somehow her knees buckled—and she was sitting once more. Not wanting to look as scared as she felt, she tried to think about something far, far away.

As far away as Whiskertown. What was Senator doing right about now?

The boy across from her tilted back in his chair. He clasped his arms behind his head. "You're friends with that girl, right?" he asked. A cluster of red pimples streaked across his chin; Quinney tried not to stare at them.

"What girl?" she asked, stalling. Her throat felt so tight that she was surprised any sound was able to emerge.

"That *Margaret* girl," the boy next to her said. "The one who was in the car accident."

"Oh, I guess you mean Marguer-*ite*," Quinney said, pronouncing the name carefully. As if that could make things any better.

"Yeah, whatever," the boy with pimples said. He leaned forward suddenly, clanking his chair down hard. "Listen," he said. "You tell her that if she wants to mess around, there's plenty of guys here who like to party."

"Right here in her own school," the other boy said.

Quinney cleared her throat and got ready to stand up again—and to make her escape. She could *kill* Marguerite for this, she thought savagely. "Well, okay, I—I'll—"

"Hey," the skinny boy with pimples said loudly. "If she's friends with Margaret, maybe *she* likes to party, too." He jabbed his finger at Quinney, and several kids from nearby tables looked over at her.

Quinney blushed and stared down at the disgusting greasy mess left on her lunch tray. And it had looked so good just twenty minutes ago, she thought, sickened.

"Nah-h-h, I don't think so," the boy next to her scoffed. "She's still a baby, practically—but hey, let's ask. Wanna party, little girl?" He spoke as if he was performing in front of a crowd—which he was, at that point.

"No," Quinney whispered.

"What?" the pimply boy said, leaning so far across the messy table that he was right in Quinney's face. "We can't hear you!"

"I said—"

"I think she said she wants to," the boy next to

Quinney interrupted, laughing. He nudged her, and Quinney shrank from his touch.

"No, I—"

"She wants to! She—"

A cool, sarcastic voice cut through their mean cackles as if with a machete. "Cut it out, Rodney," the voice said. "Pick on someone your own size, why don't you?"

Quinney looked up.

It was Cree.

CHAPTER NINE
Putting Things Mildly

"Cree Scovall," Brynn said. She leaned back against her locker with a sigh of pure pleasure.

"Yeah, Cree," Quinney said, as if it had been no big deal. She balanced her math book on her notebook, then clanged the locker shut. School was over, and they were selecting which books to bring home.

Cree was tall; he was good at sports, especially baseball and track. He moved easily, loping down Adirondack's halls like a deer. Or like—like a lion, Quinney thought. Cree was strong and capable, and you just knew he would be a tough guy to have as your enemy. Not that he ever used his toughness to push anyone around—which was probably why guys liked him as much as girls did.

No wonder Brynnie was impressed.

"What happened? And don't skip a thing," Brynn said breathlessly.

"He just told those guys to stop picking on me, that's all."

Brynn frowned, puzzled. "But why *were* they picking on you?"

"Oh, no reason," Quinney said. Angry as she was at Marguerite, she did not want to give Brynn any more ammunition to use in her campaign against her.

"So did the guys put up a fight?"

"No—they just said, 'Hey, sorry, man,' like it was *Cree* they'd been bothering." Quinney grimaced a little.

"And were lots of other kids watching?" Brynn asked.

"Some," Quinney said, remembering the circle of faces that had suddenly materialized around the little group.

"Fight!" someone had called out hopefully, but there was no fight. In fact, the bullies dissolved into the crowd in seconds, leaving only their lunchtime debris for someone else to clear away.

"Thanks," Quinney mumbled to Cree as disappointed onlookers went back to their lunches.

"That's okay," he told her, sitting down. "Hey," he said, "how come you never called me back?"

"Called you back?" Quinney said, mentally throttling the twins. "I didn't even know you called."

"Well, I did—yesterday afternoon. Some little kid named Monty said he'd tell you."

In spite of herself, Quinney smiled. "Monty's imaginary," she said.

"Are you saying I didn't call?" Cree asked, frowning.

"No—I just meant that it was one of my little brothers

pretending to be Monty. But Monty isn't real," Quinney said, feeling as though she was babbling.

An uneasy silence settled over the table, and Quinney resisted a very strong urge to chew her fingernails, a habit she'd shaken two years earlier. Did Cree still want to know why Marguerite had dumped him—was that why he'd called? Or had he heard about the accident? Or did Cree call for some other reason?

"So is she okay?" he asked softly.

That answered *that* question, Quinney thought glumly. "I—I don't know," she admitted. "I did call her like you wanted, but she never mentioned the accident, and I didn't know about it then."

"What did she say?"

"Not that much—we didn't get too far. We kind of had a fight," Quinney told him.

"Too bad," Cree said, just as the warning bell rang. "Well, I gotta go—see ya. And stay out of trouble, Killer." With those joking words Cree vanished, leaving Quinney to wonder *what* was too bad—her fight with Marguerite? Marguerite's accident?

Or the whole sorry mess?

Brynn shook her head admiringly. "You're taking it "so *calm*," she marveled. "Boy, if I were you, I'd be running through the halls singing. Your reputation is made, Quinney."

"You don't know what you're talking about," Quinney scoffed, but her heart was beating quickly. "I don't even *have* a reputation, Brynn. And I don't want one," she fibbed.

Brynn shook her head again. "It's not something you get to vote on, Quinney. It just happens."

Monday night was a busy time at the Todds' house. Mr. Todd always had papers to correct after dinner, and Mrs. Todd painted in her studio, leaving Quinney to bathe the twins, read them two stories, and tuck them in—to await good-night kisses from their mom and dad.

It was an agreement Quinney had made with her parents: a little nighttime baby-sitting in exchange for completely free afternoons. Afternoons that Quinney could spend at the library, at Whiskertown—wherever she wanted, as long as her parents knew where she was and when to expect her home. And as long as she kept up with her homework.

She had put the twins to bed and was just setting down to her homework when there was a knock at the door. "Quinney-Quin-Quin," her father said in a whisper. "The boys are finally asleep. Can I interest you in a cookie?" He felt guilty eating sweets alone, Quinney had long ago realized.

"Sure," she said. "Any oatmeal raisins left?"

"I think so," he said, trotting happily down the stairs.

Quinney sat at the kitchen table. Mr. Todd rummaged

in the chipped beehive cookie jar, jiggling it slightly with one hand.

"Yum," Quinney said as he handed her a cookie, and she started nibbling its edges.

"So," Quinney's father said. "How's Marguerite doing?"

Quinney set her cookie down. What a way to kill an appetite. "I don't know," she said, shrugging a little.

"Did she show up at school today?" her father asked.

Quinney shook her head.

Mr. Todd frowned thoughtfully as he examined his cookie. "Well, Scotty Norell made it to class," he announced grimly. "Full of beans, as usual. And he was getting a lot of mileage out of having been on the front page of the newspaper, let me tell you—tried to make himself into some kind of hero. Said they'd never pin anything on Ricky. That kid needs a serious dose of reality, in my opinion."

"Huh," Quinney said. "Well, Marguerite's not going to be any hero at Adirondack, that's for sure." And that was putting things mildly.

"No, I guess not," Mr. Todd said, his voice soft.

That was one good thing about her dad being a high school teacher, Quinney thought, biting into her cookie at last. He knew the way things really were in school.

But even he didn't have a clue as to how Marguerite's behavior had made things bad for her, Quinney, in the cafeteria today. She didn't want to tell him, either; if she did, he'd want to tell her mom, and then they'd end up talking about it until midnight.

And she wanted to keep the good part private, too. Cree's lunchtime rescue was like a shiny little jewel that would tarnish if too many people examined it. Quinney wanted to keep it hidden away.

She'd take it out later, when she was all alone.

CHAPTER TEN

Reputation

"*C*areful," Miss Mudge announced as Quinney cautiously edged her way into Whiskertown on Tuesday afternoon, making sure no animals skipped out. Whiskertown was four days away from opening, and they were already filling up with animals.

Two new puppies that looked like sawed-off hunting dogs greeted Quinney with yelps and kisses, and one tried to squeeze his way past Quinney. The dogs' long bodies and big heads looked strange atop such stumpy legs, Quinney thought, but she already knew enough not to criticize their appearance in any way. Miss Mudge acted as though each animal she came across was the most beautiful creature imaginable. She told Quinney that she'd found these two only the day before, in a brown cardboard box at a rest stop on the Northway, the long scenic highway that ran from Albany clear up to the Canadian border.

Today, two yellow pencils were punched through Miss Mudge's hair, coordinating with the bright happy-face earrings that dangled almost to her bony shoulders—

much to the fascination of the young cat she was cradling in her arms.

The cat took a swing at one of the earrings, and Miss Mudge gently scolded it. "No, kitty-kitty," she crooned. "Look over there, next to Marshmallow—who is taking a nap, so don't disturb her," she said, speaking to Quinney. "I brought them in this morning."

A raised rabbit hutch stood in the middle of one of the plywood animal pens, which was filled with a tumbling litter of puppies. Inside the hutch, the mother rabbit—a gray lop-ear—sat eating a little apart from her three babies, who were sleeping inside an old wooden box. The babies were solid colored, brown, white, and black. "Oh," Quinney breathed.

"Go ahead, pick one up," Miss Mudge said. "It's good for them to get used to being handled if they're going to be pets."

Quinney fumbled with the hutch's latch as Miss Mudge explained that these came from a summer family who had decided rabbits would not go well in their city apartment, after all. The mother rabbit appeared unconcerned as Quinney reached into the box. Instantly the babies began thrashing around on the soft cloth that lined their box. "They're flipping over like furry little pancakes," Quinney said, delighted.

Miss Mudge laughed. "They do that when they're startled—before their eyes have even opened," she informed

Quinney. "It's to keep from getting squashed by their mother when she lies down."

Quinney picked up the tiny black rabbit, who quieted right away as she held it close to her body. It nestled into her hands as if melting. "Oh," Quinney said, "look at the ears. It's perfect."

"An absolutely perfect rabbit," Miss Mudge agreed, nodding sharply as if taking credit for this. Which she could, in a way, Quinney thought admiringly, because after all, Miss Mudge had been the one to save it from being left outside to become a coyote meal.

"Now, the cats' litter boxes need changing," Miss Mudge was saying. "Also those two plywood puppy pens. I already did the first one. There's some clean shredded newspaper in that trash bag over there."

"Okay," Quinney said. She gave the black rabbit a quick nuzzle on its Y-marked nose and put it back in the box. She walked over to the supply cupboard and tied on a clean apron. She put on some rubber gloves and selected a big kitty-litter straining spoon, then she went to the rear of the store. Miss Mudge turned on the radio, and a country music star began to sing.

Behind an expandable wooden gate meant to protect them from marauding puppies, several mostly grown cats watched her with interest. The cats' leader was Senator, of course. Quinney gave Senator a mock salute with the slotted spoon and stepped over the gate.

"How's your friend—the one who was in the accident?" Miss Mudge asked as Quinney crouched to greet the cats, who quickly surrounded her.

Oh, no, Quinney thought, her hand pausing mid-stroke—not here, too. She had hoped that at Whiskertown, at least, she would be safe from having to talk about Marguerite—who had yet to reappear at school.

"Someone at the pharmacy said she was your friend, when I mentioned you were working here."

Jeez—everyone knew *everything* in Lake Geneva, Quinney thought, scowling. There were no secrets. She waded through cats, heading toward the litter boxes that lined the back of the small room, army latrine–style. "It wasn't exactly a crash," she said, trying to sound casual.

Miss Mudge snorted. "Well, I only know what I read in the newspaper," she said, "and the paper said that a car crashed into a truck, didn't it? And your friend was in the car, wasn't she? I'd call that being in a crash, wouldn't you?"

"I guess."

Quinney reached down to stroke Senator. His throat rumbled comfortingly under her hand. At least cats didn't ask a bunch of nosy questions, she thought gratefully. "Anyway, she's fine."

"What did she say happened?"

Quinney straightened up. "Nothing much," she said,

as if Marguerite had told her every detail. "She was treated and released."

"It was lucky that she didn't have to stay in the hospital."

Miss Mudge said the word "hospital" the way other people would say "snake pit," Quinney thought, smiling in spite of herself. Only two days into their acquaintance, she had already heard the harrowing story of Miss Mudge's trip to the emergency room the year before, for stitches, after breaking up a dogfight.

"I drove twelve miles to the hospital," Miss Mudge had said, "all by myself, with the blood dripping down my arm. Lots of it. *Pools* of it. And then they made me wait—just because some drunken clown had an accident with a chain saw. And I was there first! I thought I was going to pass out right on the emergency room floor."

Quinney turned to her task. Well, at least Miss Mudge had been worried about Marguerite's health and not her reputation. That was nice of her—and maybe it was a good sign. Maybe that's what other people would concentrate on, too.

Quinney leaned forward with the pooper-scooper and held her breath. Reputation, she thought, scooping—reputation was what other people said about you, good or bad. You could get a reputation for being popular if the right girls were nice to you or the right guy talked to you at lunch, and you could get a reputation as a bad girl if you got into a car with the wrong people one single, solitary day. Was that fair?

And who even cared about reputations if they were as bogus as all that?

Quinney stirred the now clean kitty litter around to air it a little, and a skinny gray cat who had been watching her intently reached out his paw and batted at her hand as if thanking her. "Aw, good boy," Quinney said, and she scratched him under the chin for a moment.

On the other hand, Quinney thought, as she and the cat worked their way down the orderly row of litter boxes, there were some kinds of reputation that meant something—that were worth having. The reputation for being a good friend, for instance, or for being a good worker.

Being a good worker was definitely easier than being a good friend. You could finish a job and go home, but with friends, you were never finished. They'd fight with you or start a fight with your other friends, or maybe they'd get bored with you, or they'd do something incredibly stupid— and you couldn't do anything about it.

With work, though, all you had to do was to do it. And working with animals was the best of all, because animals loved you no matter what. Quinney hadn't spent much time around dogs and cats, so she was surprised at what good company they were. Undemanding, no arguments—just warm fur and purrs and thumping tails.

They appreciated every little thing you did for them, too, and never complained about what you *didn't* do.

"Don't break my hear-r-r-rt, darlin'!" Miss Mudge sang out, and Quinney started in on the last litter box.

CHAPTER ELEVEN

Look What the Cat Dragged In

It was Thursday night, and Mr. and Mrs. Todd had decided at the last minute to go out to dinner. Quinney was baby-sitting the twins, as she often did when her parents went out. And they often went out. They would go to dinner, or to the movies, or even to a community meeting. They liked going anywhere, as long as they went together.

"How come your parents still go out on *dates*?" Marguerite had asked Quinney once, but Quinney didn't know how to answer her. It was difficult explaining your family to someone else.

At least her parents still liked each other, she'd thought later, remembering the last time she spent the night at Marguerite's house. Mr. Harper watched TV all alone, and when Mrs. Harper returned from her weekend job at the local Bowl-A-Lot, she didn't even greet her husband, she just looked at the empty beer cans near his chair. Mr. Harper's only comment was, "Look what the cat dragged in."

Marguerite would often say her parents couldn't stand being together, but she pretended that it didn't bother her.

Marguerite—who *still* hadn't shown up at school or called Quinney. And here it was, an entire week since the accident.

Anyway, Quinney thought, biting her lip, at least her mom and dad always allowed her to do plenty of fun stuff with the twins when they went out. They had walked over to Duell's Pharmacy earlier in the afternoon and checked out two videos of Daffy Duck cartoons. They had already eaten dinner, and now they were busy making chocolate-chip cookies from dough their mother had left in the refrigerator. It promised to be a very full evening.

"How about if we just make one great big giant cookie?" Teddy suggested. "We could cut it like a pie."

"No," Quinney decided. "I think the idea is that we just make regular cookies so we'll have something to munch on after school."

"Oh, sure," Mack scoffed. "Like leftover cookies are ever going to happen, Quinney. Especially once Daddy gets home and smells them."

"We could hide them," Teddy said.

"He'd find them," Mack said wearily.

"Anyway, if we made one big cookie it would probably end up all gooey in the middle," Quinney said, buttering the baking sheets.

"Who cares, as long as it's chocolate-gooey?" Teddy said. "Tell us again about the animals at Whiskertown," he added as he licked small sticky fingers. The boys' only job was to place the little blobs of cookie dough on the sheets—by hand, since they weren't yet able to manage dropping the right amount of dough from spoons—but they were making such a mess of it that they might as well have been working blindfolded.

Quinney made herself believe that the oven's heat would kill any germs.

"Well, there's Senator, the cat," she began.

"Tell about his ear."

"It's got a kind of notch in it, up at the top. When I asked Miss Mudge about the notch, she said it was Senator's war wound—in fact, she said that's what helped him get elected to the Senate. I think the notch was really from a cat fight, though."

"Did Miss Smudge say it hurts him?"

"Not anymore," Quinney said, sliding a tray of cookies into the oven and setting the blue plastic timer. "Not since it healed. Then there's Marshmallow, of course—and her brand-new puppies!"

72

Tuesday night, a few hours after Quinney left Whiskertown, Marshmallow had given birth to four spotted puppies with very long ears. Miss Mudge called Wednesday afternoon with the news. Quinney called Charlotte, but Mrs. Van Loon said she couldn't come to the phone.

Quinney dropped by Whiskertown on her way to the library Wednesday afternoon to see how Marshmallow was doing. The absentminded dog had turned instantly into a devoted mother, indulgent as her puppies nuzzled against her, looking for milk.

"When can we see them?" Mack asked, staring hard at the oven timer. "Are they done yet?"

Quinney smiled, knowing he was talking about two different things. "It'll be three more minutes, and you can see the puppies when Whiskertown officially opens this Saturday morning. Ten o'clock, sharp. Dad said he'd take you guys over. I'll be working there all day," she added proudly.

"I want it to open sooner," Mack said, shaking the timer a little. It gave a few extra-fast ticks, as though alarmed.

"Well, Miss Mudge says it's just not going to be ready until Saturday. She doesn't want to rush things."

The twins mulled this over. "So what other animals are at Whiskertown?" Teddy finally asked.

"There's a nice gray kitty who helped me clean the litter boxes the other day, and there are some full-grown cats who will be up for adoption, even though Miss Mudge says it's hard to place adult animals. Senator's not up for adoption—he's the boss cat at Whiskertown."

Teddy and Mack looked very impressed.

"Then there's a bigger puppy," Quinney continued. "He's sort of a goof. Someone brought him in just as I was leaving yesterday—some college kids in Saratoga Springs got him when he was really little and then couldn't take care of him, they were so busy. Miss Mudge says some people treat pets like they were fashion accessories. And she told me that a lady called yesterday about an abandoned litter of kittens out on 9N, so it'll be nice and crowded for the opening."

"Monty wants to know about the goofy puppy," Teddy reported.

"No, he doesn't," Mack said.

There it was again—usually the boys had the same opinion about everything, especially where Monty was concerned, but lately, Mack had started to disagree with his brother.

It reminded her a little of her own friendship with Brynn and Marguerite. There's another trio that's breaking up, she thought grimly.

"How do you know what Monty doesn't want?"

Teddy said, his voice wobbly.

"I would have heard."

"Well," Quinney said in a hurry, "I'll tell you about the puppy anyway. He's probably part English sheepdog, except he's got a long tail with a white tip. He's also got these big shaggy feet. It looks like he's wearing bedroom slippers. He's really friendly—you're going to love him."

"Does he bite?" Teddy asked, worried.

"If he does, it's like a baby bites. You know how babies chew on everything. You guys sure did when *you* were little."

"We still do," Mack said. "On cookies, anyway. Are they done yet?"

The timer gave its clanky ring just as Quinney opened the oven to check. They ate the cookies before the chocolate chips had a chance to cool. Cookies were best that way—especially with cold milk, they all agreed.

Later, when Teddy and Mack had bathed and were curled up in their pajamas watching Daffy Duck, Quinney got out some poster board and markers and settled down at the kitchen table. She was done with her homework and had promised to make some signs for Miss Mudge before opening day. One good thing about having an artist for a mother, she thought, was that there were always art supplies around.

Quinney looked at the list Miss Mudge had made for her.

DON'T LET ANY ANIMALS OUT!!

That was to be a sign for the front door. Another of the signs Miss Mudge wanted was for the wall above her red desk:

PET ADOPTION FEE $60
To approved homes only!
Includes spay or neuter when it's time,
all shots, a bath, and a big red ribbon.
This is a very good deal,
so don't complain!

That sounded a little cranky, Quinney thought, almost as if Miss Mudge was expecting people to argue with her. But "Choose your battles," her father always advised; Quinney wasn't going to challenge Miss Mudge on this one.

Third on Miss Mudge's list was a sign to go up near the front door of Whiskertown:

LOVE THE ANIMALS,
DON'T TEASE THEM
(How would _you_ like to be teased, anyway?)

Quinney thought that one sounded a little grouchy, too, but Miss Mudge was the boss. The next sign was a short one:

PRIVATE, DO NOT ENTER

This was for the rear, blocked-off area of the shop. "That's the place animals can go when they need some time alone," Miss Mudge had told Quinney. "They can't be expected to be charming *all* the time."

Another sign was to be shorter still:

CONTRIBUTIONS!

"Please," Quinney added, printing carefully. Surely Miss Mudge wouldn't mind her adding that. This sign was for the coffee can with the slotted plastic top that Miss Mudge had glued to a table near her desk. "We'll need all the help we can get," she had told Quinney. "Considering rent, heat, food, and whatnot."

The final sign was to be posted inside the door to Whiskertown:

THANK YOU FOR COMING. BE KIND TO ANIMALS!

"But I don't think anyone who comes to a place like Whiskertown would ever be *mean* to animals," Quinney had objected.

"You can never tell," Miss Mudge had replied darkly.

When all the signs were written, Quinney selected a metallic gold marker for the fancy border she wanted to draw around the first sheet of poster board. Daffy's sarcastic quack-voice mixed with the twins' giggles in the living room as she started to work.

Right away the phone rang.

Quinney jumped for it. "Hello?" she said, trying not to sound too eager. Maybe it was Marguerite—or Cree.

"Quinney? Honey, is that you?" her mother's voice asked.

"Uh-huh," Quinney said, a little disappointed. "Where are you? Your voice sounds all hollow."

"We're still at the restaurant—I'm using the pay phone. Are the twins in bed yet?"

"They're watching their videos. I'll stuff them into bed in about half an hour, though—don't worry."

"Because there's something I wanted to tell you, baby," Mrs. Todd said, as though Quinney hadn't spoken. She sounded serious.

"What?" Quinney asked. She cradled the receiver between her chin and shoulder, and she snapped the lid back on the gold marker.

"Marguerite's going to be moving in with us for a few days."

"*What?* You're kidding, right? *Right?*"

"Be quiet in there," Teddy called out.

"Yeah," Mack said. "We can hardly hear Daffy!"

"I'm surprised you're so upset about this," her mother said. She was obviously puzzled. "But here's what happened, Quin—I got a call at work this morning from Anita. You know," she explained, "Marguerite's mother."

Quinney nodded impatiently, as though her mother could see her.

Mrs. Todd cleared her throat. "Well, it seems that Marguerite's father is a little bit upset with her. More than a little, actually."

"He's upset with his wife, or with Marguerite?" Quinney asked. She knew the answer, but she wanted to stall for a moment—to collect her thoughts.

"Both of them," Mrs. Todd said. "But especially Marguerite. It seems that a couple of his coworkers at the paper mill made some remarks yesterday about the accident. Jokes, supposedly, but he's been taking it out on Marguerite ever since she woke up this morning. He stayed home from work."

"What do you mean, he's taking it out on her?" Quinney asked, her heart pounding all of a sudden. "Is he hitting her?" Marguerite had told her before about her dad's bad temper, but Quinney had never heard that he'd hit anyone.

"No," Mrs. Todd said. "It hasn't gotten to that point yet, but Anita is afraid it might. So she called, and we made plans for the four of us to have dinner together. Mr. and Mrs. Harper, I mean. Marguerite stayed home."

"But, Mom, I don't *want* Marguerite to—"

Mrs. Todd spoke right over Quinney's voice. "Honey, sometimes families just need a sort of time-out from each other. So Marguerite's folks ended up asking if Marguerite could stay with us for a while, and your father and I agreed. It's the right thing to do—for them *and* for Marguerite."

But not for me, Quinney thought.

"The Harpers just left to tell Marguerite and help her pack a few things for her stay. Your dad and I are about to drive over there ourselves and bring her home with us."

"But, Mom," Quinney said, finally getting a word in. "I have to tell you, Marguerite's not really my friend anymore. She hasn't even called me since the accident."

"Oh, Quin, honey, I didn't know that. I'm sorry. It doesn't really make any difference, though, not at a time like this. This is an emergency."

"But, *Mom* . . ."

"It'll just be until Mr. Harper pulls himself together, honey. Your dad and I are hoping that they can get some family counseling or something, but these things take time."

"No," Quinney whispered.

"Now, I want you to clear out a drawer or two and make some room in your closet," her mother was telling her.

"Mom!" Quinney squawked. There was no room at all in her closet, she thought angrily, and her bureau drawers were already stuffed so full that she could hardly open them without a pair of socks leaping out or a turtleneck getting jammed.

"Put a smile on your face, young lady," her mother said sternly. "Like it or not, you've got a roommate for a while."

CHAPTER TWELVE

Marguerite

"It'll be like we're sisters," Marguerite said sarcastically. "Sister Quinney."

"Shut up," Quinney muttered, catching Marguerite's eye.

Marguerite's *black* eye, that is—or rather her blue-and-purple eye. The bruises blended into a red line of stitches along her brow. The hospital had shaved off a front section of her pretty brown hair to put in even more stitches. She had brushed a long lock of hair sideways to cover the spot; she kept patting it with a gauze-wrapped hand.

Quinney realized she was staring, and looked away.

"I know how I look," Marguerite said. "Who cares?"

She must have spent the night at Quinney's a hundred times before, but this time was different. She flopped onto Quinney's guest bed as soon as she walked into the room just before eleven, flinging Quinney's beloved old teddy bear to the floor. She hadn't moved once after that, watching through narrowed eyes as Quinney stomped around the room. "It's not like I really want to be here," she said suddenly.

Quinney turned to face Marguerite. "Well, it's not like I really want to *have* you here."

Marguerite lifted her chin. "Why? Because I did something you'd be too scared to do in a million years?"

"Gee, what was that?" Quinney said, trying to match Marguerite's sarcasm. "Get my name plastered all over the front page of *The Peters Falls Press* for being such a dummy?"

Marguerite shrugged and leaned over to pick at her metallic blue toenail polish. "It wasn't our fault. It was the other guy's fault, in my opinion—he just about wrecked Ricky's car."

"Oh, poor Ricky's car," Quinney said. "Who is he, anyway? Your new boyfriend?"

"Of course not," Marguerite said coolly. "Nicky Castleton is my boyfriend. Well, he's practically my boyfriend. Ricky is just a friend."

"You sure have a lot of new friends," Quinney said. She picked up her teddy bear and set him tenderly on top of a bookcase.

"Wow, that looks so nice," Marguerite said. "You have a real talent for interior decorating."

"Hey, I'm only going along with this because Mom told me to," Quinney said.

Marguerite sniffed and started in on another toenail

while Quinney tried to ignore the flecks of nail varnish that littered the fluffy white bedspread. She flopped onto her own bed and stared up at the ceiling.

"You can quit worrying, because I'm not going to be here all that long," Marguerite told her.

"Why, what are you going to do?" Quinney asked. "Go home? I don't think so." She glanced over at Marguerite, and the look on her face made Quinney realize that she'd gone too far. "Sorry," she mumbled.

"There's nothing to be sorry for," Marguerite snapped. "I know that my dad can barely stand the sight of me now." She touched her forehead again.

Quinney sat upright on her bed. "I—I—"

"If I had anyplace else to go," Marguerite interrupted, "I wouldn't be here, would I? So let's just make the best of things." She picked up a patchwork throw pillow, clasped it to her chest, and looked around the familiar room.

Quinney stared at her. "I thought we were friends," she said at last.

Marguerite looked down at the pillow and scowled. She winced, her fierce expression having pulled a few stitches tight. "We are, I guess," she answered reluctantly.

We are, Quinney thought, surprised, not We *were* friends. A little flicker of hope warmed her chest. "Huh," she said. "Then how come you've been acting so weird lately?"

"Weird like how?" Marguerite asked scornfully. "Do

you mean when I sneaked off with those guys? I've done it before, Quinney—I just haven't told you about it. You or Brynnie, who obviously despises me now."

"I meant lying," Quinney said, refusing to let Marguerite distract her.

"I never lied to you," Marguerite stated flatly.

"Well, you did to Brynn," Quinney said.

Marguerite slammed the throw pillow onto the bed. "Look, Brynnie told me that kids at school were gossiping," she explained as if she had rehearsed this speech a dozen times, "and so I just told her that I wouldn't do anything that *you* guys wouldn't do." She aimed a small, triumphant smile in Quinney's direction.

"And you don't think that's a lie?" Quinney asked, outraged.

"Of course not," Marguerite answered. "You *would* do some of the stuff I do—if you got the chance to, and if you had the nerve."

Quinney felt her jaw start to drop, and she forced herself to snap it shut. Marguerite was just too much, twisting things around so that it would end up sounding as if she had simply taken the logical course of action. *If I had the nerve*, Quinney fumed silently. Where did she come off sounding like she was so great?

And yet—and yet there was something to what Marguerite had said, Quinney admitted. For instance, it *would* be cool if she were able to talk to boys the way

Marguerite did, so funny, and bright, and comfortable. Marguerite was fascinating, that's what she was—and what almost-teenage girl didn't want to be fascinating?

Marguerite peeked at Quinney through hair that had fallen across her face. "Well, aren't you going to say anything?"

"What do you want me to say? You obviously have this whole thing figured out."

"That's right, I do," Marguerite said, lifting her chin again.

"Then there's nothing to say," Quinney stated. "Except—that I don't believe you."

"How come?"

"Because," Quinney explained, "if you didn't feel guilty about something, you would have told me about the accident right after it happened."

Marguerite touched her row of stitches. "Gee, I was kinda *busy,* Quinney," she said, trying for some of her earlier sarcasm. She didn't succeed, though; she just looked sad. "Maybe I would have called you," Marguerite finally admitted softly. "But maybe I didn't want to. Maybe I knew you wouldn't understand."

"Understand what? That you were running around with a bunch of high school boys?" Quinney asked. "And maybe drinking?"

"Understand about anything. About my *life.*"

"Well, you're right about that," Quinney said. She

86

jumped up and turned her covers down so violently that her pillow flipped off the bed. "I *don't* understand about your life, if by 'your life' you mean pretending that a guy who's a junior in high school is your boyfriend."

Marguerite sat up straight. "Nick Castleton is a senior, and I'm not pretending," she said. "He really likes me. I can tell."

"How? Because of the way he jams you into his friend's car with a bunch of other guys to go off drinking? Like that's so romantic. Get real, Marguerite."

Marguerite shook her head pityingly. "You wouldn't know. Nicky *talks* to me. Everyone says he's bad, but deep down he's sensitive, and—and thoughtful. And plus, he's totally cute."

"Deep down," Quinney scoffed. "Deep down, *everyone* is sensitive and thoughtful. So what? It's how people act that counts."

"Like the way you're acting?" Marguerite asked angrily, tilting her head.

"Huh?" Quinney was startled by the sudden turnabout.

"You heard me, *Sister Quinney*. Look at how you're acting now, when your so-called friend is sitting here with a black eye and stitches, right after her father has just about kicked her out of the house?"

Instantly Quinney felt ashamed. She wasn't being very nice, obviously. Marguerite *was* hurting, even if she was also driving her, Quinney, nuts. "But I—I'm not still your best friend anymore, am I?"

"Yes, you are," Marguerite snapped. "Or at least you were. But I guess that's all in the past, now. Huh, Quinney?"

Quinney didn't know what to say. Was Marguerite really telling her that she still wanted to be friends—after the harsh words they'd just exchanged? It seemed so, and yet Quinney asked herself—*Do* I *still want us to be friends?*

CHAPTER THIRTEEN
The Bad Girl Blues

There was a noise outside Quinney's bedroom door early the next morning, then a brief scuffle, and then Quinney and Marguerite were awakened by a series of knocks. *"What?"* Quinney called out, annoyed. Her head ached; the endless night had been punctuated by bad dreams that seemed to rise up out of the darkness at regular intervals like the illuminated guideposts along 9N, the road that linked Lake Geneva to the outside world.

The bedroom door swung open with Teddy clinging to the doorknob, and Mack tumbled into the room. "Breakfast is ready," he said from the floor.

"I wanted to be the one to say it!" Teddy howled.

"So?" Mack said, scrambling to his feet.

"You cheater," Teddy hollered.

"You're the cheater!"

"Ahhh." Marguerite put her bandaged hands over her ears and shut her eyes tight.

"Quiet down, you two," Quinney told the twins.

Teddy and Mack pummeled each other in silence for another second, and then they stopped. "Breakfast is ready," Teddy announced, panting slightly.

"They already know," Mack informed him, smirking.

"I'm really not very hungry," Marguerite said, her eyes still closed.

"Well, it's time to eat anyway, whether you're hungry or not," Quinney told her sharply, climbing out of bed. "You'd better just get up, or else this whole thing with the twins will happen all over again—and you know it, too." The little boys were drawn like magnets to Quinney's room whenever she had company.

"You look like a monster," Mack said admiringly, eyeing Marguerite's stitches.

"Did you get to ride in an ambulance?" Teddy asked, awed.

"Oh, I can't believe this," Marguerite moaned, holding her head.

Quinney finally took pity on her. "You guys, give Marguerite a chance to get dressed for school," she said. "I'm sure she'll tell you all about the accident over a nice plate of scrambled eggs."

Marguerite groaned louder.

Mack shook his head sadly. "Mommy doesn't let us talk about stuff like that while we're eating. You know that." The twins ran out of Quinney's room and thundered down the stairs. Marguerite groaned again.

"Anyway, I'm not going to school," Marguerite informed Quinney.

"Mom's going to love that," Quinney told her.

Marguerite gave her a dirty look. "It's not my fault. I'm not ready to go back to school yet—and I never asked to come here."

"And I never invited you. But you've moved in, haven't you? You're here—so rise and shine."

"Shut up," Marguerite said, her voice muffled.

Quinney got up and opened the curtains.

Marguerite squinted mascara-smudged eyes at the sunlight that filled the room. "Ow—can't you shut them?" she begged.

Quinney tilted her head, as if considering this request. "Sorry," she finally said, "but they're my windows, and I want them open. It's a brand-new day, Marguerite—a *school* day. Rise and shine!" she said again, repeating a favorite—and infuriating—saying of her father's.

"I told you, I'm not going to school And what time is it, anyway?" Marguerite asked. She peered around for a clock.

"Six-fifteen," Quinney reported, "and breakfast is *ready.* My dad likes us all to eat together on weekdays. You know, before he has to leave for Rocky Creek. And I can tell you, if you don't get up, he'll play the Sousa marches. Loud."

"Uh-h-h-h," Marguerite moaned, finally tossing her

covers back and swinging her feet to the floor. "You people are sick."

"Stop calling us 'you people,'" Quinney said. "And, anyway, you know you love to eat breakfast. You usually eat like a horse."

"Yeah, but not so *early*," Marguerite complained. "I didn't bring a bathrobe," she said, looking over at Quinney.

"Mom lent you one of hers last night, remember?" Quinney said. Mrs. Todd's old red terry-cloth robe was draped across the foot of Marguerite's bed.

"Well, but I don't have any slippers," Marguerite said, standing up and tugging the robe on over her shiny blue nightgown.

"Then wear your socks," Quinney suggested. "But you can't come to the table barefoot. It's another family rule."

"You and your rules," Marguerite groaned. She groped under the bed for her sneakers and jammed her feet into them. "I thought this was a free country. There, are you happy?" she said, turning to Quinney. "I look like a—like a homeless person."

Well, you *are* a homeless person, aren't you? Quinney wanted to say. But she didn't. It was too close to the truth.

"You'd better brush your hair, too, while you're at it," she told Marguerite. "That's another rule." It wasn't, really—any more than wearing shoes to the table was, but why stop now? This was getting to be fun!

"Jeez, this is like being in the army," Marguerite muttered. "It was never like this when I spent the night here before."

"You were a guest then," Quinney pointed out. "And it was never a school night. Now, it's more like you said—it's like we're sisters."

"I never wanted a sister," Marguerite announced. "I always liked being an only child." But she stalked over to the bureau and grabbed her hairbrush. She swiped it through her hair a couple of times. "There, are you happy?" she asked sarcastically.

"Yes, I'm ecstatic," Quinney cooed. "Now, let's go downstairs and slurp up some of those yummy eggs."

Ready for school, Quinney opened the back door. A knife edge of icy air seemed to slice into the still-fragrant kitchen; Lake Geneva had turned cold again after its brief warm spell, which was typical Adirondack weather. Quinney checked the thermometer that her father had mounted just outside the door. It was only thirty-four degrees out.

She shivered a little, wrapping her woolly plaid jacket tighter around her. Marguerite was probably laughing by now, watching her out of the bedroom window.

Why did she get to stay home yet another day? That faker.

The grown-ups had all seemed to agree that what Marguerite needed was rest, and rest was certainly what she was going to be getting at the Todds'. Quinney's mom would arrive home from teaching nursery school in time to fix herself and Marguerite a late lunch, and then Mrs. Todd would probably work in her studio while Marguerite watched TV in the living room or took another nap until the twins got home from their Friday after-school playgroup.

Rest. I could use a rest, too—a rest from *her*, Quinney thought resentfully.

She thought back on her long friendship with Brynnie and Marguerite as she walked to school. She passed a stand of poplar, trees, called popples, locally, and their small leaves set up a tiny clatter as they shimmied in the wind. Quinney tugged her turtleneck up over her chin, pulled her jacket even tighter around her, and kicked her way through fallen leaves. *Crunch, crunch.*

The girls had grown up together in Lake Geneva—Quinney, Marguerite, and Brynn. *The Three Stooges,* Quinney's father sometimes called them. She had always been the sensible one, and Marguerite was the bravest. The first to sleep without a night-light, and the first to swim out over her head in Lake Geneva.

The sudden image of a much younger Marguerite dog-paddling triumphantly back to shore filled Quinney's mind for a moment. She had been so proud of her friend.

Marguerite laughed out loud as she churned through

the water, but then—when she'd almost reached the shore—she gulped a mouthful of water and started choking on it. And Quinney, although scared of the water, had plunged right in without thinking, grabbed her friend's wrinkled hand, and helped her to her feet.

Brynn—well, Brynnie had always been a little like the helium in the shiny balloon of their friendship. Brynnie wasn't as levelheaded as she, Quinney, was, and she definitely wasn't as bold as Marguerite, but during sleepovers, Brynn was the one who made the other two feel smarter and funnier than they did at any other time.

But although Brynn could be the one to make everything float, Quinney thought, her feelings could change fast. She either loved you or hated you; you were Brynnie's enemy or her friend.

Rainy or sunny, that was Brynn. Nothing in between.

Brynn had definitely moved away from Marguerite over the summer, and she'd tried to take Quinney with her. Quinney groaned, wondering how she would tell Brynn about Marguerite staying with her.

Brynn at school and Marguerite to come home to. Quinney almost wanted to stay outside forever, in spite of the cold.

"She's *living* with you?" Brynn screeched.

Quinney's math book slid off the pile of things in her locker, and she shoved it back in and shut the door, fast.

She leaned against her locker as though everything crammed inside might join forces and attempt an escape. "It wasn't *my* bright idea," she said. "And don't you dare tell anyone."

Brynnie crossed her heart, silent.

In language arts, Erika Koopman was waiting by Quinney's desk. "Hi," she said. Quinney could imagine Brynnie's jaw dropping—Erika Koopman, voluntarily talking to her. Erika obviously hadn't heard that Marguerite Harper, the now-famous party girl of Adirondack Middle School, had moved in with the Todds.

And just as obviously, Erika *had* heard that Cree Scovall had come to her rescue in the cafeteria the Friday before— and, after a full week's thought, figured out that she might somehow profit from what had happened.

There was no other explanation. It was only the second week of school, but already Quinney knew that Erika's every move was designed to further advance her popularity. She was a girl who would never start a conversation with someone new unless she wanted something, so Quinney felt in control of the situation. She felt amazingly relaxed, in fact.

"Hi, Erika," she said, sitting down.

Erika adjusted her chartreuse chenille sweater and smiled. She brushed off a desktop and perched on one corner of it, ignoring its startled owner. "So, how's Cree?" she drawled, as if she and Quinney were good gossipy friends. "I didn't know you guys were so *close*," she added with a metallic smirk.

"We aren't close at all," Quinney said to her. Don't you dare blush, she told herself sternly.

"Aw, you're blushing. That's so cute," Erika said, clapping her hands silently, a specialty of hers. "She's blushing," she informed the rest of the class, just in case they hadn't been watching or listening.

Mr. Laurence strode into the classroom, checking his watch. Cigarette ash made the front of his navy blue sweater look as though he'd been using it as a dusting cloth. "Take your seats, everyone," he said, and he started to take roll. Erika smirked at Quinney and waggled her fingers at her—another specialty—and went to sit down.

It was all because of what had happened with Cree in the cafeteria—which had been a fluke, really.

An accident. Cree didn't really *like* her. He hadn't spoken to her since then.

Well, Quinney thought gloomily, just wait until everyone at school found out that Marguerite was her roommate. Better enjoy being popular while you can, she told herself, because the bad girl blues are going to catch up with you again before long. . . .

CHAPTER FOURTEEN
Are You Jealous?

Erika Koopman wanted to talk with Quinney after school that day. "Let's go hang by the lake," she said, leaning against the bank of lockers next to Quinney's.

This was another first. "I don't know," Quinney said, glancing over at a nearby group of girls—the ones Erika usually hung out with. "I'm supposed to help out at the library today. Mrs. Arbuckle is expecting me."

"Let her expect you," Erika said, laughing. "You have better things to do. Bring her, if you want," she added, jerking her head toward Brynnie, who was standing shadowlike next to Quinney. "I'm going to tell my friends I'll see them tomorrow. This is private—there's something I want to ask you."

Aha, Quinney thought. Now she'd find out what Erika wanted.

She tried not to worry about poor Mrs. Arbuckle, the librarian, who might be standing at the red library door about now, searching for her in vain. Quinney was supposed to help arrange the book sale rack today, but that chore would have to wait. An afternoon like this might never happen again. *I'll make it up to you, Mrs. A.*, Quinney vowed.

She thought Marguerite would approve of her decision. But she didn't know how that made her feel.

The three girls ended up at the green picnic tables in the little park next to the lake, where the seventh and eighth graders lolled on warmer days. Sixth graders inherited the park only when the weather turned cold, Quinney knew—the coolest sixth graders, anyway.

Erika grabbed a bag of cheese curls from her backpack and passed them to Quinney, and Quinney passed them on to Brynn. They ate for a while, licking orange-colored cheese salt from their fingers.

"So, my birthday's coming up in a couple of weeks," Erika finally said.

"Oh. Happy birthday," Quinney told her.

"In advance," Brynn added with unaccustomed bravery.

Erika ignored her and continued speaking to Quinney. "And I kind of wanted to give a party, but I wanted to ask some boys. Nice ones."

Like Cree, Quinney thought.

"And since you're such good friends with Cree Scovall

and all," Erika was saying, "I thought maybe you could find out if he and some of his friends want to come. To the party."

"That sounds like fun," Brynn said enthusiastically. She looked at Quinney with pleading eyes. Don't tell her no, she seemed to say.

Erika turned to Brynn as if surprised she was still sitting there. "Oh, I'm sorry—*you* can't come," she said, as if stating an obvious fact. "There isn't room. I was going to ask Quinney, though," she added.

Brynnie shrank back as if Erika had slapped her.

Furious, Quinney jumped to her feet. "I'm going to be busy that night," she told Erika. "And so is Brynn, and so is Cree, probably. Come on, Brynnie—it's freezing. Let's get out of here." Brynn got off the table and walked over to Quinney as though hypnotized. They started to leave.

"But—but you don't even know when my party *is*," Erika objected. "How can you say you're going to be busy?"

"I can just say it, that's all," Quinney called over her shoulder. Next to her, Brynn was in tears; Quinney felt like strangling Erika.

"I was trying to be nice," Erika yelled after her. "Oh, go ahead and bring Brynn, if it means that much to you."

"Too late," Quinney sang out. "We have better things to do. *Whenever* your party is."

"Where have you been?" Mrs. Todd asked the moment Quinney walked through the back door. She turned from washing her paintbrushes in the sink, and a lock of brown hair fell into her eyes. She tried to blow it away with a loud *foof.*

Quinney glanced up at the kitchen clock: five-thirty already. She put her bookbag on the table and tried to look as if this had been an ordinary afternoon. "I don't know," she said. "Just walking home." And blowing off Erika, and trying to calm Brynn down.

"Well, Mrs. Arbuckle called," Quinney's mother said. "She was worried about you." She looked at her daughter for a moment and frowned, indicating her concern.

Mrs. Arbuckle! With everything that had happened, the fact that she had ducked her library responsibilities had completely slipped Quinney's mind. "Huh," Quinney finally said, trying to look puzzled. "I thought I'd told her I couldn't make it today." She reached blindly for an apple.

"Well, you didn't. You're going to have to call her up and apologize. I have her home phone number right here."

"Okay," Quinney said meekly. She thought of the cheese curls roiling around in her stomach—and the apologetic phone call she had to make sometime that night—and she put the apple back in the bowl. She opened the refrigerator and pulled out a carton of juice. "So, where are the twins?" she asked casually, trying to turn their conversation away from the events of the afternoon.

Mrs. Todd laughed. Teddy and Mack were famous for bounding into the kitchen whenever the refrigerator door opened. "They're in the studio," she said. "Marguerite is painting their faces for them."

Quinney choked on some juice. "She's what? Where?" she asked, astonished. For one thing, her mom hardly ever let anyone into her studio. And for another thing—Marguerite? Playing with Teddy and Mack?

Quinney's mother laughed again. "You heard right," she said. "She thought it might be fun, and so did the twins, and so she got face paint over at Duell's. They've been in there for ages."

"But—but—"

Mrs. Todd reached for some paper towels to dry her brushes. "Why are you so surprised?" she asked.

"Because Marguerite doesn't even like little kids," Quinney blurted out. "She's absolutely thrilled being an only child—she even told me so."

Her mother's eyebrow shot up. "People aren't all one way or all the other, honey. Marguerite can like being an only child and still enjoy playing with your little brothers occasionally."

"But she never wanted to before," Quinney argued, putting her juice glass down with a bang.

"Well, she's doing it now," her mother said, shrugging. She frowned a little, holding the clean brushes up to the light as she shaped their damp bristles.

"But, Mom." Quinney couldn't believe her mother's attention could shift so quickly.

"Why, Quinney, are you jealous?" Mrs. Todd asked, gazing at her daughter in surprise.

"No," Quinney said stiffly. "I just don't want her getting paint in their eyes and stuff. They could get hurt—she's not very experienced. With kids, I mean."

"Oh, for heaven's sake." Mrs. Todd shook her head.

"Well, don't say I didn't warn you."

"I must say, young lady, that I'm a little—"

But before her mother could say the words *disappointed in you*, which Quinney knew were coming next, the back door opened. In came Quinney's dad, accompanied by a gust of cold fresh air and a few swirling leaves.

"Norman," Mrs. Todd said, looking overjoyed. She held out her arms for his hug.

As if her father didn't come home this time every evening, Quinney thought, embarrassed. She turned away from their embrace, but her parents were like that.

A moment later the twins burst into the room through the swinging door that led to the studio. "Daddy," they squealed, hurling themselves at their father.

Marguerite appeared in the doorway, head tilted, witnessing this scene as if—as if she were watching a TV program, Quinney thought.

"Watch out for the paint," Marguerite warned Mr. Todd.

"Whoa," he said, laughing. He held his sons away at arms' length.

"Look at me, Daddy—I'm a kitty," Teddy said. Sure enough, he had a black-painted nose, orange and brown tiger stripes, and fine black whiskers decorating his face.

"And I'm Frankenstein," Mack shouted. *"Grrr,"* he growled, holding out pretend monster hands. Marguerite had painted dark circles under his brown eyes and a crudely stitched gash along his forehead. A trickle of fake blood dripped from the corner of his mouth. "I have stitches just like Marguerite."

"You guys look terrific," Mrs. Todd told the boys.

"Marguerite painted us," Mack informed his father.

"I'm going to school like this on Monday," Teddy announced. "No baths for me."

"Me neither."

"Sorry, you can't go to school all painted up," their mother told them. "Maybe on Halloween, though."

Teddy ran over to Marguerite and grabbed one of her hands. "Will you still be here on Halloween?"

Marguerite glanced up, catching Quinney's eye. "Probably not," she said, looking away. "But I only live three blocks away. I could come over and paint you guys for trick-or-treating, if you really want."

"I really want, I really want," Mack said, jumping up and down.

"What about Monty?" Quinney asked, wanting to join the conversation—and to bring up something Marguerite knew very little about, if anything at all. "What's *he* going to be for Halloween?"

"Monty?" Teddy said, surprised. Quinney usually told the boys not to talk about their invisible friend in front of guests.

"He's just pretend," Mack said, his voice pitying as he looked at Quinney, who, to her fury, blushed.

Marguerite couldn't hide her laugh.

"You really did a good job, Marguerite," Mr. Todd said, gazing at the boys.

Marguerite shrugged. "I always liked doing makeup and stuff. I just never tried it on little kids before."

"Well, you could do this at harvest festivals and fund-raisers and so on, honey," Quinney's mom said. "People would pay good money—they always have face-painting booths at places like that. You should give it a try."

Marguerite shook her head slightly.

She *had* always been great with makeup, Quinney admitted to herself, trying to be fair. "You should, Marguerite," she chimed in, a little late. "You should try it."

Marguerite shot her a look. "I'll think about it," she said—in a way that Quinney knew meant the subject was closed. Marguerite would *never* paint faces again.

Unless she happened to feel like it.

CHAPTER FIFTEEN

Adverbs

"Okay, bye, Mrs. Arbuckle—and thanks. It won't happen again, I promise. See you Wednesday." Quinney hung up the phone, relieved that that little ordeal, at least, was over.

Since it was to be such a full weekend, and since her parents were a little miffed with her for blowing off the library that afternoon, Quinney was instructed to work on her homework after dinner even though it was a Friday night. But not too much homework was getting done.

Quinney sat on her bed, with notebook, textbooks, and papers spread all around as if they were a second quilt, and she tried to make a list of adverbs. Instead, though, she found herself peeking at her onetime friend. Marguerite wasn't even pretending to do anything important; she merely sat on her own bed, legs folded, filing her fingernails.

"Stop staring at me," she told Quinney.

"I'm not," Quinney said, looking away. *Rapidly, quickly,*

sneakily, Quinney thought, glancing at her homework.

Grouchily.

"Yes, you are too staring," Marguerite said, but without any energy.

Lazily. Quinney added the word to her list. "Well, you're getting fingernail dust all over my room," she said, and then she sighed. She wiggled her pen back and forth so fast that it became a blur. "Forget about it. It's not that important, I guess. What I really wanted to say was—"

"Don't," Marguerite snapped.

Quinney's pen stopped moving. "Don't what?"

"Don't say you're sorry for the way you've been treating me," Marguerite said, "because it won't make any difference. So you might as well save your breath."

Quinney's heart *thunka-thunked* in her chest. "I wasn't going to apologize," she objected, although that had been her intention. Sort of.

"Yes, you were," Marguerite said, "but only to make yourself feel better. You may think I'm bad, but at least I mean it when I say I'm sorry."

The accusation hit Quinney in the face like a water balloon. "I don't think you're *bad,*" she objected. Outside the Todds' house, a cold September wind was blowing. Leaves fell from trees and brushed against Quinney's windows with a quiet *tick, tick* on their way to the ground as if counting the seconds between the girls' sentences.

Marguerite shrugged. "My dad thinks I'm a bad girl,"

she said, her voice almost steady. She pulled her long brown hair back into a ponytail, then let it fall around her shoulders. "He's even called me worse than that."

Quinney didn't want to hear whatever it was Marguerite was about to say.

"And he doesn't even know what happened that day," Marguerite continued. "But that's not a problem for him. Oh, no."

"I—I'm sure he didn't mean anything by it," Quinney stammered.

"How could he not mean anything? He meant *everything* by it," Marguerite shot back. She twisted a strand of hair and pulled it, hard. "Anyway, it's none of his business."

Quinney closed her notebook. "But it *is* his business," she objected weakly. "After all, he is your father."

"And so he gets to criticize me and call me names?"

"Well," Quinney said, "I guess he—"

"Don't take his side," Marguerite interrupted. "He never cared what I did before, so why should he start caring now?"

Quinney looked away. What Marguerite said was true; Mr. Harper hadn't ever seemed to care much what Marguerite did. It was as though he was living in a separate zone from Marguerite and her mother, Quinney thought, even when watching TV and drinking beer—lots of it. Which he was usually doing—when he was at home, anyway. And yet he had called the Todds' house three times already since Marguerite had arrived. "Well, maybe he was upset because of what happened to him at work," Quinney said.

"What happened at work?" Marguerite asked, obviously puzzled.

Quinney's breath caught in her throat. Marguerite hadn't heard.

"What happened at work?" Marguerite persisted.

"Oh, well, my mom said that some guys at the mill teased him about you, or something," Quinney mumbled. "But maybe she got it wrong."

The color rose in Marguerite's face. "I don't believe you," she finally said. "I didn't even do anything."

"Don't act so surprised," Quinney said, suddenly stung by Marguerite's words—because where did Marguerite get off assuming that nothing she did affected anyone else? "Lots of people are suffering because of that stupid accident, you know."

"Well, it's none of their—"

"It is their business, whether they want it to be or not," Quinney interrupted. "It's *my* business. I'm the one those seventh-grade guys ganged up on in the school cafeteria, aren't I?"

"What?" Marguerite goggled at Quinney.

"It's not just you-you-you all the time," Quinney said, furious. "No matter how much you want it to be. What happened to you happened to your family and your friends, too."

"You don't even know what *did* happen to me," Marguerite objected. "You don't know what I was thinking when I got in that car."

"Who cares what you were thinking?" Quinney snapped.

Marguerite scowled at her.

"Well, what were you thinking?" Quinney asked, calmer.

"I was thinking maybe I would have some fun for a change—with some people who really liked me," Marguerite said.

"With high school guys who were *drinking*?" Quinney challenged her.

"Maybe they were and maybe they weren't. So what? It was great—until that other guy hit us."

"The paper said it was your car that ran the stop sign."

"That's not the way I remember it," Marguerite said flatly, but then she smiled. "I was kind of distracted, though—squashed up next to Nicky like that. I think he really does like me, Quinney."

Quinney stared at her, silent. Marguerite was too much.

"You shouldn't have asked the question if you didn't want to hear the answer," Marguerite said, shrugging. Then, in a seemingly casual voice, she asked, "So, what happened to you in the cafeteria?"

"Like you really care," Quinney scoffed.

"I *do* care," Marguerite said quietly. "What happened?"

Now Quinney was the one to shrug. "They tried to mess with me. Oh, and I'm supposed to tell you there are plenty of seventh-grade guys who want to party, if you like it so much," she said, trying to keep her voice light.

"Those jerks," Marguerite said. "Like I would. Did everyone hear?"

"Enough kids heard," Quinney said. She picked up a battered math book, opened it, and let it flop shut a couple of times. "Did you really have fun—before you got hit, I mean?"

Marguerite stretched. "Yeah, it was okay. At least it was something to do," she said. "Jeez, I hate this town."

"But, Marguerite," Quinney said, leaning forward urgently. "You're never going to get out of Lake Geneva if you keep on goofing up this way."

"That sounds like Brynn talking, not you," Marguerite said with a bitter laugh. "Typical Brynnie. She hates my guts."

"No, she doesn't," Quinney said "At least, she didn't use to."

"But she does now?" Marguerite asked quickly.

Quinney didn't know what to say; she wasn't sure she knew the answer.

"Huh," Marguerite said.

"I think she's just worried, that's all," Quinney mumbled.

"Well, she doesn't need to be."

"It's not that easy. You can't stop caring about your friends—just like that."

"I still care about you guys, too," Marguerite said, her voice softening. They looked at each other and almost smiled. "It's just that—oh, I need my life to be exciting. You know that. Those older guys like me, and they're just—well, they're *fun*."

The moment of connection was gone. "I'll bet," Quinney scoffed. "Marguerite, didn't you ever ask yourself why Nick Castleton would want to hang out with a twelve-year-old girl?"

"I'm almost thirteen," Marguerite objected. "And I look a lot older."

"Oh, come on."

"He likes me," Marguerite insisted. "I know what you're thinking, but that's not what it is! We've never even kissed yet."

Though Quinney was surprised, something in Marguerite's voice made her, Quinney, believe she was telling the truth.

Marguerite swung her feet to the floor and rested her elbows on her knees. "Look, do you want to know what happened that afternoon?" she asked. "I mean, what *really* happened?"

"Yeah, I do."

"Okay," Marguerite said. "Okay," she repeated, as if

she was setting her thoughts in order. "Well, I decided to bail from school right after lunch, and I bumped into Nicky on my way home—in front of the market."

"By accident?" Quinney interrupted. "The market's not exactly on your way home from school."

"Half by accident," Marguerite admitted, grinning a little. "I guess I know some of the places where he hangs out when *he* cuts school."

"Okay," Quinney said, feeling like a prosecutor on a TV detective show. "So you bumped into Nicky Castleton in town. And then what happened? How did you end up in that other guy's car?"

"Well, we had to wait forever for Scotty to show up, and then we were all laughing and stuff, and we just piled into Ricky's car. I guess the guys thought if they really wanted to relax they'd better get as far out of town as possible."

Relax? More like drink, Quinney thought. "And they invited you to go, too?"

Marguerite blushed a little. "Kind of," she said. "They didn't seem to mind if I went, and I didn't want to say good-bye to Nicky yet, and so . . . "

"And so . . . " Quinney prompted.

"And so the next thing I remember is being in that ditch. The doctor said I probably had a slight concussion." She looked away, then stretched and yawned with great delicacy.

Just like one of the cats at Whiskertown, Quinney thought suddenly. "Huh," she said. She could sort of see how something could happen like that, though—how you could climb into somebody's car, and then before you had time to think about it much, it might be too late.

But there was something that Marguerite wasn't telling her—Quinney knew it. "Hey," she said, forcing Marguerite to look at her. "Tell the truth."

The good thing about the game was that it sometimes made you blurt out something real, even if you didn't know it was real before you said it.

Marguerite grimaced. "Okay," she said at last. "You know after the accident? After that truck hit us?"

Quinney nodded, not bothering to correct Marguerite this time.

"Well, I do remember something. Nicky didn't seem to care if I was hurt or not—not really," Marguerite said softly. "He was just worried about his dad finding out."

Quinney didn't say anything or ask questions; that was the only rule to the game besides telling the truth. But Nick Castleton's lack of caring was Marguerite's worst injury, she knew.

"It was still fun, though," Marguerite said, looking stubborn. "I'm not sorry I went."

Oh, right—it sounded like fun, Quinney thought scornfully. But she didn't speak.

"Now, you," Marguerite said. "Tell the truth." Her look

challenged Quinney to dig really deep for her reply.

"Okay," Quinney said slowly. "Well, I guess maybe if I was all-of-a-sudden talking to—to someone I liked, some boy," she clarified, thinking immediately of Cree Scovall, "and if some friends of his came by in a car," she continued, "and if they asked us to get in, I might get carried away and do it. That's a lot of ifs, though."

"But you can see how it might happen," Marguerite said, excited.

"Yeah, kind of," Quinney grudgingly admitted. "But that doesn't mean it wouldn't be a dumb thing to do, Marguerite."

Marguerite inspected her fingernails as if her manicure was her most important concern. "Don't tell anyone—what I said about Nicky not caring, okay? Not even Brynn. Especially not Brynn. Because Nicky does care about me, Quinney—I'm sure of it."

"Okay, I won't," Quinney said. She picked up her ballpoint pen and turned back to her list of adverbs.

Slowly, determinedly.

Sadly.

CHAPTER SIXTEEN

The Grand Opening

S aturday morning was cool and sunny, and a steady breeze stirred up ripples on the surface of the Hudson River and Lake Geneva. It was a perfect day for the grand opening of Whiskertown.

Quinney arrived two hours early, as planned, but Miss Mudge had gotten there even earlier. She opened the door for Quinney, who was struggling to hold the posters upright against the wind. She'd gotten up at six to finish them.

Miss Mudge's face was pink with excitement, and rhinestone-studded chopsticks were jabbed into her shiny black hair at an extra jaunty angle. She was wearing a new T-shirt, and it had the word *Whiskertown* printed on the front in bright red rounded letters. Wavy black whisker lines curled out from each end of the word. "There's one for you to wear," she told Quinney gruffly. "I got a few made up." She gestured to several teetering stacks atop her file cabinet.

"Here are the posters."

"Thanks—and have a doughnut," Miss Mudge said. "I bought six dozen in Peters Falls." She made this announcement with an air of someone who had journeyed to Paris.

A large urn of coffee bubbled and perked on Miss Mudge's desk, filling the shop with its fragrance, and a big bunch of red helium balloons bobbed above her desk chair. Senator watched the balloons, fascinated, while the half-grown sheepdog-mix puppy crouched and barked at the unfamiliar objects.

"Puppy, no," Quinney scolded gently.

"Forget about trying to keep him quiet," Miss Mudge said. "He's been barking for an hour already. Dog has the brains of a field mouse—no offense to field mice."

"Oh, don't say that," Quinney objected. "I think he's kind of smart, really. He's never seen balloons before—but he *knows* he's never seen them. That's why he's barking."

"I *guess* I see what you mean," Miss Mudge said. She grabbed a roll of silver duct tape and started putting the posters up here and there down the length of the long rectangular room.

"I think this only proves what a good watchdog he'll make for someone," Quinney said.

They both turned to stare doubtfully at the half-grown dog, who had stopped barking only long enough to make a puddle on the floor. "Let's just hope that person doesn't have a carpet," Miss Mudge said, pounding a ragged strip of tape flat with her fist.

"I'll mop up after him."

By nine thirty, the red balloons swayed in front of Whiskertown, Quinney's signs were all up, and—much to the big puppy's interest—two large trays of luridly colored doughnuts—pink, green, and blue frosted, with various sprinkles—had been carefully placed on Miss Mudge's bright red desk.

Quinney had to keep rearranging the doughnuts as her boss helped herself to first one, then another, then another. "I'm a nervous eater," Miss Mudge announced proudly.

The animals were ready for the grand opening, too. The brown, black, and white baby rabbits were nestled in their freshly lined wooden box like furry Christmas presents, and next to them, the gray lop-eared mama rabbit cleaned herself energetically, as if preparing for the curtain to go up.

In the first enclosure, Marshmallow's snowy fur gleamed with brushing, and she watched proudly over her litter; the puppies were getting cuter by the day. Quinney had made a last-minute sign for their box:

RESERVATIONS NOW BEING TAKEN
FOR MAMA AND PUPPIES

Quinney gave the excited young sheepdog a good scratch behind his hot shaggy ears; as a thank-you, he licked her face with so much enthusiasm that Quinney had to push him away. "His mouth is a lot cleaner than yours is," Miss Mudge called from across the room.

"If you say so," Quinney replied, laughing, and she gave the sheepdog an extra hug. She tied a bright blue piece of yarn around his neck, and he occupied himself for the next few minutes by turning in circles, trying to get a good look at it. Miss Mudge shook her head at this display.

The litter of orange kittens occupied one of the raised enclosures against the wall. Their little tails tapered to points, and it looked as though they were wearing striped soccer socks, Quinney thought. Freshly brushed and well fed, some of the six tumbled around, fighting mock battles, while the others slept.

Senator had taken up his position on a table near the front door, ready to greet whoever might walk in. He looked dignified. His long tail curled neatly around his feet, hiding them.

At the rear of the shop, behind the expanding fence, the skinny gray cat who had helped Quinney clean the litter boxes was curled up on the velvet sofa. He watched all the activity with big eyes. "He's excited about the opening," Miss Mudge said, looking pretty excited herself.

There was a knock on the door. "Not open yet," Miss Mudge called out, her voice muffled by a pink-iced doughnut flecked with shreds of coconut.

"I'll go tell them," Quinney said. She opened the door a crack and found herself staring right into a big arrangement of flowers. Queen Anne's lace; mop-headed, bronze-colored chrysanthemums; and a few late sunflowers vied for space in the lavish arrangement.

"Sign here," a voice said, and a clipboard was pushed in her direction.

"Miss Mudge, I think they're for you," Quinney called out, not sure what to do. Floral deliveries weren't at all common in Lake Geneva; most people gave friends arrangements from their own gardens. In fact, Quinney thought, the nearest florist shop must be more than half an hour away, in Saratoga Springs. What kind of tip would this delivery man expect?

Miss Mudge stalked to the door, scrawled her name, crammed a dollar bill in the man's waiting hand, and practically shoved him out the door. She snorted as she read the card that was attached to the flowers. "Hmmph, it's David. Again."

Could Miss Mudge possibly have a boyfriend? "Um— David who?" Quinney asked, trying to sound casual.

"David-the-Vet," Miss Mudge said, putting the vase on her desk. "You'll meet him—he's coming here today. He used to help me out with the animals."

"In Vermont?" Quinney prompted, when it became clear that Miss Mudge was not going to provide any more information.

"That's right."

"And he's coming all this way?"

"Quinney, give it a rest—it's only a couple of hours' drive. He probably just wants to make sure his silly flowers arrived," Miss Mudge said. She tweaked a nodding sunflower until it was just perfect, though.

Only ten minutes to go . . . which was good, Quinney thought, because there weren't going to be many doughnuts left, not at the rate Miss Mudge was eating them.

It seemed to Quinney that everyone in town came to the opening of Whiskertown. Well, it had been years since a new business opened on Main Street. The day was a blur of excitement filled with noisy barks, tiny meows, and the sudden pop of balloons. There was also Miss Mudge's occasional piercing cry, "Quinney, rags!"

All the doughnuts were gone by eleven thirty.

Teddy and Mack were among the first to arrive, accompanied by their father. "Hi, guys, hi, Dad," Quinney said. "Let me introduce you to Miss Mudge. Oops," she added, as the puppy dashed out the door, which the twins had left open.

"I'll get him," her father said. He soon reappeared, the panting sheepdog trotting happily alongside him as Mr. Todd gripped its collar.

"Look at his tongue," Mack said, amazed. "It's so floppy."

"And so *pink*," Teddy added.

"He's a good boy," Quinney's father said. "Just a little

overly enthusiastic, that's all."

"What's his name?" Teddy asked.

"Rags, Quinney," Miss Mudge said quietly as a puddle started to spread.

"Good boy, Rags!" Mack said.

Marguerite showed up right after her father and the twins left, to Quinney's astonishment. She had cut some super-short bangs in an attempt to disguise the place where the hospital had shaved her hair; only on Marguerite, Quinney thought, would that look good. Marguerite was with two high school kids Quinney didn't know, a boy and a girl, and she seemed to be showing off for them—and for the entire town. Several people whispered to each other at the sight of her; Quinney didn't know whether to greet her or pretend to be busy.

"Oh, look at the kittens," Marguerite said loudly, open-ing the enclosure door and lifting one up to her still slightly bruised face. Her short tight sweater rose up high on her midriff; the kitten batted feebly at Marguerite's nose.

"Don't let it scratch your eyes out," the other girl cried, shrinking back in an exaggerated way.

Quinney strode over to where the little group was standing, wanting to rescue the kitten before Miss Mudge noticed what was going on. "Hi, Marguerite," she said, plucking the kitten from her. She restored it to its mother.

"Oh, hi, Quinney," Marguerite said. She acted as if she were surprised to see Quinney there. "These are my friends," Marguerite added, but she didn't introduce either of the two kids by name.

"Cute T-shirt," the high school girl said to Quinney, not looking like she meant it. She smirked at the boy.

"Thanks," Quinney said coolly. Using her one free hand, she tried to straighten the oversized shirt as best she could.

"Oh, you're welcome," the girl said, grinning. She and the boy wandered off toward the door.

Marguerite gave Quinney a tiny smile, shrugged, and followed them.

Quinney turned away.

Other people liked the Whiskertown T-shirts better. "Are they for sale?" one woman asked.

"Yes—we're taking orders," Miss Mudge said, instantly appearing at Quinney's side. As the T-shirt requests mounted up, Miss Mudge made an announcement: "Twelve dollars for the T-shirt, twenty for the sweatshirt. Twelve dollars for the apron, and eight for the hat."

"I didn't know you had that many things printed up," Quinney whispered.

"I didn't, but I'm going to now," Miss Mudge replied, eyes agleam.

Cree Scovall came in just as Marguerite and her friends were leaving; Cree and Marguerite ignored each other, to Quinney's secret delight. "Hey, Quin," Cree said, coming over to her.

"Oh, hi," Quinney said. "Sorry you missed the doughnuts."

"That's okay," Cree said. He melted into the crowd.

Mrs. Arbuckle, the librarian, came in just after one o'clock. "Quinney, how wonderful everything looks," she said. She scratched Senator under his fuzzy chin, and his rumbling purr was audible even in the crowded room. "What a fine big fellow you are," she said to the cat. "Oh, I do love pussycats."

"We have some fine *little* fellows over here," Quinney said, leading her to the orange kittens. Quinney opened the cage door. She couldn't even see Cree now, but she heard him laugh. Well, she thought, at least he was having a good time.

"Oh, look," Mrs. Arbuckle said, clasping her hands. The kittens were putting on a show for their admirers— pouncing on one another, chasing their own tails, or simply shutting their eyes and mewing pitifully. They sounded a little like the seagulls that sometimes made it all the way up the Hudson River from the Atlantic Ocean, wheeling and crying. "Oh," Mrs. Arbuckle repeated, scooping up a tiny complaining kitten and cuddling it to her chest. It attached itself to her mint green sweater like an awkward corsage.

Teddy and Mack reappeared with their mother just after one thirty. "I had to come over and see this for myself," Mrs.

Todd said. "Whiskertown is all anyone could talk about at lunch. Here, honey," she added, slipping Quinney a brown paper bag. "I packed you a couple of sandwiches—egg salad and tuna. And where is Rags, by the way? The boys especially wanted me to meet him."

Charlotte came by at about two o'clock. She pushed her way over to Marshmallow's enclosure, Quinney behind her, and the dog thumped her tail in frenzied greeting. The chewed spot on her tail was almost healed. Brynn joined them a few minutes later.

"Brynnie—thanks for coming," Quinney said. "Did you see Marshmallow's puppies yet?"

"Nuh-uh," Brynn said, sounding shy. "That's a darling dog, Charlotte."

"Thanks," Charlotte said, pleased. "Quinney and I saved her life, probably."

The front door swung open with a *whoosh*, and an extremely tall man automatically ducked his head as he entered the crowded room. Quinney worked her way through the crowd in time to see him greet Miss Mudge.

"Hello, Edith," the man said. "I see you got my flowers."

Miss Mudge nodded abruptly. "They look expensive," she said. "We always need *donations*, David, the next time you feel so inclined."

He took an envelope out of his jacket pocket and jammed it into the coffee can on her desk. "I'm making a donation, too, but I wanted you to have the flowers."

Miss Mudge blushed, then turned to Quinney, who was watching the two of them as if hypnotized. "Quinney, don't you have something to do?"

"Huh? Oh yes. I'm sorry, Miss Mudge," Quinney said. She was just about to join Brynn and Charlotte, who—much to Quinney's surprise—were talking animatedly to one another, when the door opened again.

There stood Mrs. Van Loon.

CHAPTER SEVENTEEN

Trouble

It was obvious that Mrs. Van Loon meant to make trouble. She looked around the crowded room and licked her thin, lipsticked mouth almost hungrily. In spite of the crowd, she spotted her daughter over by Marshmallow's enclosure at once. Quinney saw Mrs. Van Loon's usual composure slip for a moment, and she thought the woman might actually howl with fury.

Unaware of her mother's arrival, Charlotte was showing one of the puppies to Brynn. Mrs. Van Loon worked her way over there—fast.

Quinney was even faster. "Charlotte," she warned. "Look out! Your mom—"

Charlotte's eyes widened, and she handed the puppy to Brynn with trembling hands. But Mrs. Van Loon turned to Quinney, not to her daughter. "I might have known you were behind this, Mary McQuinn Todd."

"Behind what?" Quinney said bravely, although her

heart was pounding. "All I did was help find a home for a dog you didn't want."

Cree materialized behind Quinney. He stood there silently, as if ready to defend Quinney, Marshmallow, and the puppies.

"You went behind my back," Mrs. Van Loon almost growled. She beamed a quick, public smile around the room for those who might be watching, and Quinney felt goose bumps break out on her arms. "And as for you," Mrs. Van Loon added, turning to her daughter. "What do you mean by sneaking out of the house on a Saturday afternoon when there's work to be done?"

"I didn't sneak," Charlotte objected weakly. "I left a note saying when I'd be back."

This did not appease her mother. "And I suppose you didn't know that dog would be here?" she said, gesturing toward a cowering Marshmallow. "After telling me she'd run away?"

So Charlotte and her father hadn't told Mrs. Van Loon about taking Marshmallow to Whiskertown, Quinney realized. Well, she didn't really blame them.

"I—I *did* know Marshmallow was here, Mother," Charlotte admitted, her voice sinking to a whisper.

Mrs. Van Loon aimed another everything's-fine smile around the room. "And what about your father? Did he know, too?"

"What seems to be the problem?" a stern voice asked. It was Miss Mudge, followed closely by David-the-Vet.

"Are you the owner here?" Mrs. Van Loon asked, looking Miss Mudge up and down in a nasty way. Mostly up, because she was so tall.

"I am," Miss Mudge said. "And I take it you're the wife of Marshmallow's *former owner*." By this time, half the people in the shop had gathered around them to watch what was happening. The other half was listening—but pretending not to.

Cree shifted his balance from one foot to the other, still ready for action. Quinney was standing so close to him that she could feel his warmth. She would never forget his bravery, she knew.

"That's right, I am," Mrs. Van Loon said, a tight smile on her face. "And you're in illegal possession of this animal. My daughter had no right to give her to you. Obviously you intended to make a nice little profit from the dog," she added, gesturing toward the pet adoption sign Quinney had made.

"First," Miss Mudge said. "That adoption fee doesn't *begin* to cover my costs here. Dr. Havers can bear me out on that." She jerked her head toward the vet, who nodded gravely. "Second," she continued, "I have a signed release from Mr. Van Loon that hands ownership of Marshmallow and her puppies over to me."

Mrs. Van Loon gasped. "I—I don't believe it," she finally sputtered.

Now he's in for it, Quinney thought, almost sorry for Mr. Van Loon. Almost.

"Quinney," Miss Mudge said. "My desk. Top right drawer." Quinney scurried off toward the red desk.

"And third," she heard her boss say in her high, clear voice, "Mr. Van Loon only signed that paper because you said you were going to have Marshmallow destroyed. *Killed,* along with the puppies," she emphasized to the entire room.

Now it was the crowd's turn to gasp. They looked from Mrs. Van Loon to the nursing puppies, and back again.

It was clear that their sympathies were with the puppies.

Grasping this fact at once, Mrs. Van Loon tried desperately to defend herself against the charge. "I—I would never have said I was going to do that if Marshmallow hadn't been such a vicious animal. She's a bad dog."

Marshmallow cringed at the words *bad dog*, and shifted her shivering flank in an attempt to cover her puppies. Cree moved one step closer to the enclosure.

"I wouldn't be at all surprised if the pups turned out to be dangerous, too," Mrs. Van Loon said, turning to the people gathered around her. "I certainly wouldn't advise anyone to adopt one, and I ought to know."

"Mother," Charlotte said, her voice shaking, but loud enough for everyone to hear. "That's not true—

about Marshmallow being vicious."

It was the bravest thing Quinney had ever seen Charlotte do. She wanted to cheer.

"That's right," Miss Mudge chimed in. "Marshmallow is one of the sweetest dogs I've ever had the pleasure to meet. She's a good mother, too," she added, raising an eyebrow at the angry woman. *Unlike some people I could mention.* The words hovered unspoken in the crowded room.

"That dog growled at me twice," Mrs. Van Loon announced, her cheeks flushing dark. "You can't tell *me* she's a good dog."

"Not only is she a good dog," Miss Mudge said. "She's obviously also a good judge of character." The crowd laughed at this remark, to Mrs. Van Loon's increased fury.

"Let me see that release form," she snapped.

Quinney handed it to Miss Mudge, who held it up for the woman to read. Quinney half expected Mrs. Van Loon to grab the paper and rip it to shreds, but she only scanned it quickly, then made a noise that sounded like a snort. This was quickly followed by a look of horrified disgust, and she stared down at her feet.

There squatted the sheepdog puppy, calmly spreading yet another small puddle across the floor—and onto one of Mrs. Van Loon's large sandaled feet. Cree laughed out loud, and the other onlookers soon joined in, relieved at having such a satisfactory conclusion to this upsetting exchange.

"Rags, Quinney," Miss Mudge said, barely able to hide a smile. "No hurry though, dear," she drawled. "Take your time."

Mrs. Van Loon shook her foot, turned, and stormed out of Whiskertown. She paused only long enough to whirl around and shout, "Charlotte!" over her shoulder.

Charlotte ducked her head and scurried after her mother.

"Hmmph," Miss Mudge said, looking after them. "It's a pity we can't get a release form signed for that poor girl as well."

CHAPTER EIGHTEEN

Brynnie

Whiskertown's grand opening was a triumph, in spite of Mrs. Van Loon. Two baby rabbits were adopted, and three orange kittens also had new homes, two of them together. In addition, more than a hundred dollars had been donated to Whiskertown, most of it from Dr. Havers, Quinney suspected, and six T-shirts sold.

"Today was so much fun," Brynn said as she and Quinney walked slowly down a nearly deserted Main Street. On an ordinary Saturday night Quinney and Brynn might have continued on to the Todds' house—for dinner and maybe a sleepover. In the old days, Marguerite would have joined them.

But having Marguerite actually living at her house changed all that, Quinney reflected.

Still, she didn't want the happy day to end; she was going to walk Brynnie home and then double back to her own house. "Yeah—everything went pretty well, considering," she agreed with a sigh.

Brynnie grinned and looked quickly around, as if someone might be eavesdropping. In front of the market, Mrs. Bloom was sweeping scattered leaves and candy wrappers into a tidy pile; she waved hello to the girls, who waved back. "It was so cool that Cree Scovall showed up—and he didn't come to see Marguerite either, if you ask me," Brynn whispered when they were safely past.

"Well, Cree's all right," Quinney said, shrugging, but a big smile betrayed her true feelings.

"I think he likes you, Quinney," Brynn said solemnly.

"No—we're just friends. But that's good enough." For now, she added silently to herself. In a year or two, who knows?

"Good enough? It's great!" Brynnie said. "I wish I had a friend like that."

"I wish you could come over tonight," Quinney said in an attempt to change the subject.

"Oh, me, too—but Sam is taking my mom and me out to dinner in Peters Falls. Maybe even a movie, so at least I won't be bored."

Quinney smiled again. Sam Weir—eccentric, talkative, and even rich, at least by Lake Geneva standards—had been her most difficult listening customer over the summer. But then he'd met Brynn's mom. They'd only been dating for a few weeks.

"That'll be fun," she told Brynn. "I'm jealous, even. Marguerite was so rude at the opening, and now I'll probably have to go home and spend the whole night listening to her explain why it wasn't her fault."

Brynn shook her head in sympathy, and her blond hair caught the late afternoon light. "So, what's it like actually living with her?"

"Messy," Quinney said, after thinking for a moment.

"Huh—I might have guessed," Brynn said, half laughing and half snorting her disgust. "She always was kind of a slob."

"Oh, like we're so neat," Quinney said a little uneasily. She had her own problems with Marguerite, true, but it didn't feel right ganging up on her.

Even after the way she'd acted at the Whiskertown opening.

"You're neat, but she's even worse than me," Brynn said. Then she turned to Quinney, her face almost hidden by shadows. "Everybody's number one topic of conversation. Here, let's sit down—we're going to run out of time before we run out of talk." The girls ambled over to the bench next to the town's tennis courts. They were near the end of Main Street just where the road turned a little shabby, kinking off toward the river—and Brynnie's home on River Road. The girls brushed away a few stray leaves from the initial-carved bench and sat down. Above them, although it was still light out, a floodlight ticked as it went on and began its steady buzz.

"I don't think Marguerite wants to be the main topic of

conversation," Quinney said, trying to be fair.

"Oh yeah? What about the time the three of us got lost when we went for that walk last winter?" Brynnie asked. "You and I got cold, right? But poor tragic Marguerite, she nearly froze, to hear her tell it."

"Well, I guess she does kind of exaggerate a little," Quinney conceded. "But—"

"A little? What about when everyone in the fifth grade got the flu last spring? We were all sick, but Marguerite just about died."

Quinney remembered how it had annoyed her at the time.

"Well, I'm fed up with it," Brynn announced, kicking savagely at the leaves gathered under the bench. "And I'm sick of everyone giving her all this attention just for being bad. What about us? Who ever pays any attention to us for being good?"

Quinney chewed her lower lip. She wanted to argue with Brynnie because, after all, Marguerite was getting bad attention, too. Just look at the way her dad was acting. And when it came right down to it, how much attention did Marguerite *ever* get at home—where it counted?

On the other hand, Quinney had to agree with Brynn a little bit. After all, weren't her own mom and dad bending over backward to be nice to Marguerite, even letting her move in with them? And hadn't all this happened because of that stupid accident?

"Say something," Brynn said.

Quinney shrugged. "I guess it's natural for people to be kind of worried about—"

"I'm not worried," Brynn interrupted. "Marguerite deserves whatever happens to her."

"But maybe that's what we should talk to her about," Quinney said urgently. "And you might be the only person who can help, Brynnie."

"Me?" Brynn stared at Quinney. "Why me?"

Quinney didn't know quite how to put it. "Well," she began slowly, "remember what you told me the other day—about how Marguerite was going to get in trouble— get pregnant, I mean—if she wasn't careful?"

"Just like my mom did when she was in school," Brynn confirmed, nodding.

Quinney sighed heavily, relieved that Brynnie had been the one to say the words. "Yeah, I remember you told me that," she said. "Anyway, I was talking with Marguerite last night, and—well, the thing is, she doesn't seem to be sorry or anything—for what happened. She'd probably do it again even, if I know her."

Brynn shrugged. "Probably. Doesn't surprise me."

"So I was thinking," Quinney continued, "maybe you could talk to her—tell her what it was like for your mom to have to get married when she was still in high school, and what it was like getting dumped by her so-called husband just when she needed him most. She knows how hard your mom has had to work all the time and stuff, but maybe you could tell her the details. Tell Marguerite what it's like to be—to be—"

"To be trash?" Brynn asked coolly, using Marguerite's own cruel word.

"I never called you that."

"It's what you meant, isn't it?" Brynn snapped. "You want me and my mom to be like a civics lesson to Marguerite—*what not to do with your life.* And you're thinking how terrible it would be for your precious Marguerite to have a baby too soon—a baby like me?" Brynnie was almost crying now.

Quinney jumped to her feet, her throat tightening with sadness at the hurt she'd caused Brynnie, who was usually so sweet.

Brynnie, who Quinney had practically ignored all summer long. "No, I only meant—" Quinney stammered.

"Look, you just don't get it, do you?" Brynn interrupted, her face even paler than usual.

"I guess maybe I don't," Quinney muttered.

"Okay, I'll spell it out for you," Brynn said. "Things change, Quinney. You don't want them to, but they do. It's like—oh, it's kind of like the river, see?" She gestured helplessly toward the tangle of bushes and trees that hid the Hudson—all but a couple of gleaming silvery puzzle pieces.

The river?

"My mom says the river is changing all the time, and she's right—even when it looks like it's holding perfectly still." Brynnie tilted her head, and a last shaft of sunlight outlined her hair.

Quinney pictured the Hudson River, still wild and clean as it flowed through the town of Lake Geneva. Even when the river was at its glassiest and most quiet, she thought, as it was so many heavy, hot days during the summer, it was moving—covering the miles between the summer camps of rich visitors and Brynnie's house and the first paper mill downstream in Marathon as if it was no distance at all.

"The river changes," she agreed reluctantly.

"You can't pin it down, no matter how pretty it looks at any given moment," Brynn said. "Even if you want it to stay just that way."

"Yeah, but what—"

"So maybe it's like that with friends, too," Brynn interrupted. "I think you want things to stay the same as they always were, Quinney. You and me and Marguerite, the three best friends, like always. You don't want me to be mad at her, and I'll bet you wish she'd start being nice to me again. Isn't that right?"

Quinney didn't answer, but she had to admit to herself that Brynnie was right.

"It's a pretty picture, Quinney, but everything has changed," Brynn said, shaking her head. "Things haven't really been the same for almost a year. The summer was the end, for me—when Marguerite started acting all bored with us and everything."

"But—"

"Look, stop trying to force us to do what you want, okay? Jeez, that's probably why you like taking care of those animals so much, isn't it? But we're not your little Whiskertown pets, Quinney. Marguerite's different now, and so am I. And so are you! You're always off doing something now—you're never around. You're never *there* for me anymore—hey, you've even got a boyfriend, now. Sort of."

"I do not," Quinney said, blushing furiously.

"You can't control everything," Brynn said. "I hate Marguerite now, see? I just hate her for—oh, for having a mother and a father and *still* messing up. I hate her for all the clothes they buy her, and all the chances she gets. And I hate her for making fun of me."

"But you guys used to be—"

"*Used-to-be*, Quinney. Yeah, we used to be friends, but we aren't now. Get over it! You have to let me hate her. And I am *not* going to talk to her about my mom and me. You're asking way too much from me." Brynn was crying by the time she finished speaking.

"Okay," Quinney said, shaken. "Okay, sorry—it was just a thought, Brynnie. Do you forgive me for asking?"

"I guess," Brynn said, wiping her cheeks dry with her sleeves.

"I won't do it again," Quinney promised.

"Well," Brynnie said with some of her old spirit. "You'd just better not, that's all."

After walking Brynn to her front door, Quinney slowly made her way home. The balloons, doughnuts, and flowers of Whiskertown's festive opening seemed to belong not simply to another day—but to another lifetime.

I messed up with Brynn, Quinney thought sadly as she opened the back door.

The kitchen lights were on, but the only person in the room was Marguerite, who was sitting cross-legged under the wall phone. Her skinny black jeans looked as though they'd been sprayed onto her legs, they were so tight. "Okay, bye, Mom," Marguerite was saying as she twisted the phone cord. She looked at Quinney and rolled her eyes expressively.

Oh, now she wanted to be friends, Quinney thought scornfully. *Quack, quack, quack*; the voice on the other end was barely audible from where Quinney stood.

"Okay, bye," Marguerite repeated. She pulled her knees to her chest and stretched her big white sweatshirt over them.

Quack, quack, quack.

"I really gotta go now, Mom," Marguerite said, getting to her feet. "Quinney needs to use the phone."

"No, I don't," Quinney called from across the room—

loud enough, she hoped, for Mrs. Harper to hear. She didn't want to be used like that.

"She's kidding, Mom—she's kidding. Quinney, cut that out!" Marguerite called out playfully, but she shot Quinney an angry look. "Bye, Mom. I love you, too."

Marguerite had cupped her hand to the receiver when she said these last words, but Quinney heard them anyway.

"Where is everyone?" Quinney asked, as Marguerite scrambled to her feet and hung up the phone.

"Shopping for tomorrow," Marguerite said, flipping her hair over her shoulders.

"Why, what's tomorrow?" Quinney asked blankly.

"Family outing," Marguerite said, as if quoting someone. "And oh boy, I get to come," she added in her most sarcastic voice.

Quinney's heart dropped an inch or two. "I forgot all about it," she said, although her parents had been trying to do something as a family each Sunday, weather permitting. It was their new policy.

"Well, start remembering," Marguerite said coolly. "Your supper's in the fridge, by the way. It's some kind of casserole—you're supposed to heat up your plate in the microwave. Your mom said she's sorry dinner was so early. She meant to tell you."

"Nobody ever tells me anything around here," Quinney said, stomping over to the refrigerator and pulling out her dinner plate. Peas, carrots, and something white lay smashed under plastic film; she tried not to look too closely.

"Poor Quinney," Marguerite cooed.

"Shut up."

"What's with you, anyway?" Marguerite asked. "I thought you'd be all psyched and everything, after your grand opening." She said the words a little sarcastically, Quinney thought.

"Why'd you even bother to come if you were just going to make fun of it?" Quinney asked, pushing microwave numbers with angry jabs.

Marguerite blinked, surprised. "I didn't make fun."

"Well, your friends did."

"I can't help that," Marguerite said reasonably. "And, anyway, they aren't really my friends—I just bumped into them, kind of. At Duell's. I liked Whiskertown, Quinney," she added suddenly. "Really, I did."

"I don't believe you," Quinney mumbled, pulling her plate out of the microwave.

"Why would I lie?" Marguerite asked. "Someone's got to take care of the strays in Lake Geneva. Just ask your mom and dad—they're taking care of me, aren't they?"

CHAPTER NINETEEN

Bear Slide

"But how much longer is she going to be here?" Quinney asked her mom early the next morning. The two of them were alone in the kitchen for the moment, piling up sandwiches as fast as they could make them. Marguerite was still in bed, grabbing a few extra minutes of sleep. Mr. Todd was upstairs with the twins, helping them get ready for the family outing.

"I'm not sure," Mrs. Todd said. "Her mother and father have an appointment in Peters Falls tomorrow morning, but I wouldn't get my hopes up if I were you. Mr. Harper is just barely going along with the idea of seeing a counselor."

"But Marguerite's the one who's acting crazy, not her parents," Quinney objected. "And she doesn't even think she's been doing anything wrong."

"I'd hardly say she's acting crazy," Mrs. Todd objected. "Just because she's been running a little wild. And she will talk to the counselor. Probably next week."

"But how come her parents are going?"

"They all have to talk to someone because it's considered a family problem," Quinney's mother said. "It's really none of our business, darling."

"It is *my* business," Quinney muttered. "I'm the one who has to share my bedroom, aren't I? I don't see you and Daddy inviting her to crawl in with you."

"Quinney, be generous," her mother said, cutting a stack of sandwiches into triangles and then bagging them. "I think it's doing Marguerite some good staying here. She's eating and sleeping pretty well, and she's being great with the twins."

"Yeah, but what about the rest of us? How are *we* doing?"

Mrs. Todd put down her knife. "Oh, we'll survive," she said. "But she'll be going back to school again tomorrow, so she'll need a little extra support, Quinney—from you."

"Well, I'm not walking to school with her," Quinney said.

"Guess what, Quinney?" Teddy asked, barreling into the kitchen.

"What?" Quinney asked automatically, half expecting him to answer "That's what," which was the twins' most recently discovered witticism.

"I'm going over to play with Jeremy after school tomorrow," Teddy said instead. Jeremy was the twins' new kindergarten friend. Quinney had met him once already, and the twins talked about him all the time.

"You are? That's neat," Quinney said.

"And you know what, Quinney?"

"What, Teddy?"

"Mack's not coming." Teddy looked excited, proud, and scared, all at the same time.

"You mean he's doing something else?" she asked.

Teddy shook his head. "No, I guess he's just staying home. He wasn't invited." His dark eyes searched hers as if looking for some answer.

"How come?" she asked. "Is there some problem between Mack and Jeremy?"

Teddy nodded, solemn. "They had a fight. Yesterday, after we took Mommy to Whiskertown."

"You missed the whole thing," Mrs. Todd told Quinney.

"But you guys fight all the time—you and Mack," Quinney said. "You and Mack and Monty, too. What's the big deal? You're always squabbling about something."

"Yeah, but Mack and Jeremy *really* had a fight yesterday."

"You mean they hit each other?" Quinney couldn't picture it; Jeremy seemed so shy, the time she'd met him anyway.

And Mack—while argumentative lately—defended every snail against being crunched, every fly against being swatted.

She turned to her mother, but Mrs. Todd shook her

head as if she didn't want to get involved. She started washing some apples.

Teddy nodded his head and glanced nervously at the kitchen door, watching for his brother. "It all started with this hole we were digging in the backyard."

Quinney remembered the project—the twins had been talking about making a swimming pool for a couple of weeks now. Quinney's parents had finally approved, hoping to end up with a miniature pond in which the boys could sail toy boats.

"So what did they fight about? Who would get to use the shovel first?" Quinney asked.

"No, they fought about who owned the hole," Teddy said. "Mack said we did, because it was in our yard."

Silent, Mrs. Todd inspected an apple.

"What did Jeremy say?" Quinney asked, curious.

"He said nobody could own a hole, because a hole is nothing. It's invisible. Then he said it was exactly like Monty, because Monty was invisible just like the hole, so nobody could own him. And Marguerite said that made sense to her."

"Wait a minute," Quinney said. "Marguerite was there, too?"

"She showed up partway through the fight," Teddy said. "She said she'd just ditched her high school friends because they were so boring. And that's when Mack got mad."

Marguerite hadn't told her anything about ditching the

high school kids. But I didn't give her a chance to say much, Quinney admitted to herself. "And Mack hit Jeremy?"

"First he yelled at him," Teddy explained patiently. "Then he told him to get off his property. But Jeremy just stood in the hole and said it wasn't his property, it was a hole. And, anyway, it was part his, because he helped dig it, so *that's* when Mack hit him."

"And what were you doing all this time?"

"I was just watching. It all happened kind of fast."

"Did Mom break it up?"

Teddy glanced at his mother, who held another apple up to the sunlight streaming in through the window and inspected it. "No, Marguerite did," he said. "They were all dirty from rolling around, but she told them fighting wasn't cool. Mack got sent upstairs to take a bath, and Daddy took Jeremy home. Then Jeremy's mom called last night and talked to Mom, and that's when I got invited over. All by myself. And then we went shopping," he added.

"But this is terrible!" Quinney exclaimed. She wasn't sure if she was more upset about the fight itself, Marguerite stopping the fight, or the fact that no one had told her about it until now.

"These things happen," Mrs. Todd observed. "It's time for each of the twins to start branching out on his own. It's not a bad thing, Quinney."

It sure seemed like a bad thing, Quinney thought. The

148

twins always did stuff together—with invisible Monty as their most loyal companion.

"Jeez, Mom—it's like Marguerite is hijacking my whole family," Quinney said after Teddy had left the room. "What business is it of hers if Mack gets into a fight? Why didn't anyone ask me what I thought?"

"Quinney, what on earth is the matter with you?" Mrs. Todd asked, exasperated. "You weren't here. What were they supposed to do, keep on fighting until you got home?"

"But that doesn't mean Marguerite had the right to—"

"That's enough," Mrs. Todd said firmly. "Go get ready, honey. Today is going to be fun."

Yeah, right, Quinney thought.

The dirt trail leading up to the area known as Bear Slide was steep, and everyone panted a little during the climb. Teddy and Mack scrambled up the trail first, herded by their father as if they were lambs. Quinney followed silently, while her mother and Marguerite trailed farther behind, chatting intermittently. "I've never been up here," Quinney heard Marguerite say.

The trail leveled off at the top of the hill, winding its now-rocky way through rustling trees. Even though it was a warm Sunday afternoon, there were no other hikers around; this part of the Adirondacks was never very crowded.

What everyone called Bear Slide was really an immense

exposed granite slab left behind by an ancient glacier. Its surface stretched as far as Quinney could see, sloping gently up the shady hillside.

Maybe the whole mountaintop was simply one big rock, Quinney thought, looking around. If so, parts of that rock had broken up over time, and Teddy and Mack jumped from one flat chunk to another—now acting more like mountain goats than lambs. Quinney's parents kept an eye on them while admiring the little plants that lined the narrow path—lichens, starry mosses, sweet ferns. The broad slide's dark surface was smooth, and a green slick grew under the thin skin of water that flowed down its center crease. This is what made the slide as slippery as an icy sidewalk in places. Here and there, though, the water gathered in little pools.

Eventually, Quinney found herself alone with Marguerite, who was shaking a pebble out of her sneaker. "Pretty up here, isn't it?" Quinney said, balancing on a rock.

"It's okay."

Quinney sighed and looked around. I really don't know what to say to her anymore, she thought uneasily.

"I want to eat over there, on the other side," Mack yelled from atop a rock that seemed to have been squared off by some giant hand.

"You can't," his mother called out. "You'd have to be able to fly to get over there."

"Maybe he can," Teddy said hopefully. "Go ahead—try!"

Marguerite started to giggle, a pretty sound that seemed to echo the moving water. Quinney smiled in spite of herself.

"No, he *cannot* fly," Mr. Todd shouted. "Mack, you stay right there."

"Find a nice spot where we can have our lunch," Mrs. Todd urged the little boys.

"We'll let you take off your shoes and socks and wade after we eat," Mr. Todd said.

It had been years since Quinney and her family had been to Bear Slide, although it was only five or six miles away. Quinney and her parents had often picnicked there before the twins were born. They'd never been sliding, though—that was for teenage daredevils.

But maybe her mom and dad had done it when they were kids. Quinney smiled at the thought.

"What are you grinning at?" Marguerite asked, clutching at a branch to steady herself as they worked their way over to where Mrs. Todd was unpacking the lunch basket.

"Nothing."

"I want my own private rock to eat lunch on," Mack announced loudly.

"But I want to eat lunch with you," Teddy said, voice wobbly.

"We'll all eat together," their father said. "Even though privacy is usually my middle name."

"I thought Homer was your middle name," Teddy said, perplexed, and Marguerite giggled again.

Mrs. Todd started distributing the sandwich packets.

"So how come we haven't been up here in ages?" Quinney asked her parents when things had settled down. They were seated on adjoining granite slabs in the dappled sun; Quinney's rock even had a mossy little hummock she could lean against. It was just like a pillow. She took a bite of her tuna sandwich.

"Oh, your mother had this thing about the twins, when they were babies," Mr. Todd told her. "She didn't want to see them go shooting off down the slide like a couple of acorns. But they're older now."

"I'm keeping my eye on them, though," Mrs. Todd said.

"Now you, on the other hand," her father continued, "you were a sensible child, Quinney. When we used to bring you up here, you would warn *us* about being careful."

"Didn't I ever do anything even a little crazy?" Quinney asked, frowning up at the leaves over her head. It sounded as though she had always been so—so boring.

"Never," Marguerite said lazily.

"Oh, I wouldn't say that," Mr. Todd corrected her. "There was this one time . . ."

"Tell me," Quinney urged.

"You were about three years old, as I recall," her father said. "You and your mom and I climbed up here to have a picnic. You'd packed the lunch, of course, Quin, after checking the weather report and figuring out the quickest and safest way to get here."

"Oh, Dad." Honestly—she'd only been a toddler, after all.

"So after you guided us up the trail and cleaned up the picnic things, you told your mother and me to take a little nap. You were going off for a nature walk, you said."

"Uh-huh," Quinney said, amused. Her father loved telling tall tales.

"So, the next thing we know, this big old black bear comes sliding down the mountain on his rump, in front of our very eyes! He passed right by me—I had to duck out of the way. I was terrified, I don't mind telling you—but he was even more scared."

"A bear?" Mack asked, electrified with excitement.

"And do you know what that bear was saying as he went scooting by?"

"No, but you're going to tell us, I have a feeling," Quinney said. This should be a private family story, she thought, sneaking a look at Marguerite, who appeared to be dozing. Would Marguerite make fun of it—and them—later?

"He said, 'Oh, save me, *save* me from that wild, crazy, and totally unpredictable kid—she tried to pull my little tail!' And then he was gone." Mr. Todd lowered his voice dramatically before speaking again. "And to this very day this place has been called the Bear Slide in honor of that poor creature's effort to save his tail—from you, kiddo."

Eyes still closed, Marguerite smiled.

"Yay-y-y-y!" Teddy cheered. Mack eyed his sister with new respect.

Quinney sighed happily. "Well, as long as I wasn't always the boring one. It's nice to have a history."

"You've got more than a history; you've got a reputation. Up here, anyway," Mr. Todd said.

"Then I'm glad we came," Quinney said.

"Me, too," Marguerite said, eyes still shut.

CHAPTER TWENTY

Civil War

The next morning Marguerite dressed carefully, clearly intending to make a big impression her first day back at school. It would be a grand entrance. No disappearing into the woodwork for her.

Quinney watched her squeeze into her tightest black Levis and shrug the cropped black denim jacket she loved over a snug red T-shirt. Marguerite's new short bangs looked spiky, even a little challenging. "What are you staring at?" Marguerite asked.

"Nothing," Quinney said, giving her own hair a few quick extra strokes with the brush. She was dreading the walk to school, but she knew her mom would be watching them closely for any signs of discord.

Oh sure, Quinney admitted to herself. Marguerite had acted pretty nice up at Bear Slide the day before, and sure, she hadn't said anything mean—or anything much, for that matter—last night before bed. She had seemed unusually quiet, in fact, almost wistful.

But who knew how long her good mood would last?

That's what her mom didn't understand, how Marguerite could turn on a person in an instant. That, and how bad things probably would be at school—for Marguerite, and for anyone seen hanging around with her.

"What are we waiting for?" Marguerite asked, as if she knew what Quinney was thinking. She even smiled, almost challengingly.

"Nothing," Quinney said. "Let's go."

The girls walked along Church Street without saying a word. Quinney felt sorry for Marguerite, having to face everyone after all the gossip, but it was her own fault, wasn't it? She kept her head tucked down as she walked, as if that might make her invisible.

"I'll walk in front of you if you want," Marguerite said coolly. "Your mom's not watching anymore. She'll never know."

"No, that's okay," Quinney said, blushing a little.

They crunched through a stretch of fallen leaves without speaking. "I guess I don't mind so much that kids have been talking about the accident," Marguerite finally said. "But does everyone know that my dad kicked me out of the house?"

"He didn't kick you out," Quinney protested. "He just needed some time alone with your mom. Time to think."

"Same diff," Marguerite shrugged, lengthening her stride.

"Well, Brynnie is the only one who knows you've been living at my house," Quinney told her as she struggled to keep up.

It's not like *I'd* go around telling people, she added silently. Trust Marguerite to see this whole thing only from her angle.

"And we all know how loyal Brynnie is. To me, anyway," Marguerite said, the corner of her mouth twisting up in a sarcastic smile.

Quinney didn't say anything.

Their steps slowed as they reached the outskirts of school. A shaft of light broke through the clouds, making the low-slung school gleam almost golden for a moment. "There it is," Marguerite muttered, half under her breath.

"Everything will be fine," Quinney said, echoing her mom's optimistic parting words.

Marguerite flashed Quinney a look of contempt. "Things are not going to be fine," she said. "And you know it."

Quinney blushed. Things were going to be fine for *her*, at least. If she had any control over the matter. "Maybe it won't be as bad as you think," she said weakly.

Marguerite looked weary all of a sudden. "Give it up, Quinney. And don't look so worried—I'll try not to embarrass you any more than I already have. See you second period." And without a backward look, she strode off toward school.

Leaving Quinney standing on the sidewalk all alone.

"I hear she's actually back at school," Erika Koopman was saying as Quinney took her seat, waving a silent hello to Brynn. As before, there was no need to specify who was meant by the word *she*.

"I saw her, and it doesn't even look like she was in an accident," Carla Hopsinger said. Her pale face wrinkled a little. She looked disappointed. "Does she have a hidden scar anywhere?" she asked, turning to Quinney.

"How should I know?"

Erika snorted. "She's living with you guys, isn't she?" she asked. She narrowed her eyes, challenging. Clearly Erika was still miffed that Quinney had stood up to her after school the week before. Now was her chance to get even.

Quinney turned around and shot Brynn a dirty look. "I didn't tell," Brynnie muttered.

"Why," Erika taunted, "was it supposed to be a secret or something?"

"I heard her parents kicked her out," Carla said excitedly.

This was exactly what Marguerite had most dreaded. "They did not kick her out," Quinney said. "They just needed some time." She looked around for Mr. Laurence, but he was still outside smoking.

Give it up, Mr. Laurence, Quinney raged silently.

"They kicked her out," Erika said, nodding so decisively that her black curls bounced. "I don't blame them."

"Well, I think it's kind of harsh," Carla said, surprising Quinney, because usually Carla automatically echoed whatever Erika was saying. Erika shot her a look, and Carla shrank back, chastened. "But maybe not," she amended.

"I don't blame them for kicking her out," Brynn said, lifting her chin defiantly.

"They didn't kick her out!" Quinney said, raising her voice a little.

Erika looked from Quinney to Brynn, then back again. She clapped her hands without making any noise. "Oh, excellent, a fight," she said, gleeful. "And you two are such good friends!"

"We are not having a fight," Quinney said loudly, just as Mr. Laurence entered the room, trailing cigarette fumes, as usual.

"There will be no fighting in *this* classroom," Mr. Laurence said, aiming a frown in Quinney's direction. "Now, get out your lists of adverbs, people."

And Erika laughed—delightedly.

Moments before second-period history class was to begin, Marguerite swept into the room with all the confidence of a movie star. "Hi, everyone," she drawled, flinging herself into her assigned seat without once looking Quinney's way.

So that was how it was going to be, Quinney thought uneasily. Marguerite was leaving it up to her.

"Hi," a couple of kids murmured back. A few of her classmates stared at Marguerite with undisguised curiosity, while others simply looked embarrassed.

"I like your hair," a girl called out. She sounded a little sarcastic, though. Two other girls whispered and then giggled, but Marguerite quelled them with a glance.

"Miss Harper," Mr. Foster called out, looking up from his desk. "I was sorry to hear about the accident. Thank goodness you're all right. There's a lot of work for you to make up, I'm afraid. You missed most of the Civil War."

"That's what you think," Marguerite said softly, flashing Quinney a look.

The Civil War, when the country divided into warring factions, friends slaughtering onetime friends with an unexpected ferocity.

Just like the three of us, Quinney thought suddenly. Quinney-Brynnie-Marguerite, once a team. Now split apart forever.

"Well, Quinney can help you catch up," Mr. Foster said. All eyes turned to Quinney at this remark, and Quinney felt herself blush. She was furious. What was this? Had someone posted an announcement by the front door saying that Marguerite was now practically part of her family?

Everyone continued to look at Quinney, and a couple of girls were whispering, staring at her as if seeing her for the first time.

This was not fair, Quinney thought. Maybe some kids were thinking she had gotten into the car with those guys too, if she and Marguerite were such close friends.

She was the one who messed up, Quinney thought angrily—and now, thanks to Marguerite, she, Quinney, was messed up.

At a brand-new school.

"I—I—doubt very much that I'll be able to help Marguerite," she announced formally, in a loud, ringing voice that startled even her.

Marguerite froze.

Mr. Foster looked up, surprised. "Oh? And why's that?"

"Because we're not really friends anymore."

There was a heartbeat of silence, then a few kids started whispering. Already regretting what she'd said, Quinney didn't dare to look at Marguerite. "Quiet!" Mr. Foster snapped, and the whisperers were still. "See me after class, Marguerite," he said, his voice softening. "I'll make sure you get all your assignments. Now, let's proceed with Reconstruction."

At lunch Quinney dawdled as long as she could at her locker, hoping that the cafeteria would be so crowded by the time she finally got her lunch that there would be no question of sitting with Marguerite—if Marguerite would even consider sitting with her, that is.

And if she hadn't ditched school.

Quinney worked her way slowly through the cafeteria line, selecting first a gelatinous glistening mound of macaroni and cheese, then a tiny dish of salad, the iceberg lettuce browning at the edges, then a plastic cup of red Jell-O with a banana slice suspended in it. The little piece of fruit looked surprised, as if wondering, How did this happen?

Quinney sympathized. She felt the same way about what she'd said in Mr. Foster's class. She'd been pushed into it!

There was no way of making things right, though.

Maybe the whole disaster would just blow over.

Yeah, sure.

Quinney grabbed a container of milk and shook a few ice chips from its waxen sides. "Hey, watch it," the girl next to her said as a little piece of ice landed on her tray.

Quinney hovered at the doorway of the noisy cafeteria and tried to survey the room as if she weren't really doing so. At one table Erika was surrounded by her usual group. She picked disdainfully at her lunch, but she was managing to eat most of it, Quinney noticed.

At another table Rodney and the heavier guy, her tormentors, were screeching insults at each other while other seventh- and eighth-grade boys egged them on. Every so often Rodney looked around, as if searching for someone.

Quinney shrank back in the doorway just as a milk carton flew through the air. A harried-looking lunchroom monitor rushed over to Rodney's table to see what was going on.

There was no sign of Cree.

At the end of another table—the only one left with empty seats—sat Marguerite, who was slowly eating a cup of fruit-flavored yogurt with impressive languor. She didn't seem to notice Quinney or to be paying much attention to Rodney and his friends.

That's why those boys were acting up, Quinney realized in a flash. They wanted to impress Marguerite, the school's new bad girl, but they were too chicken to come right up and talk to her.

There was an empty chair across from Marguerite, but her long legs were stretched out, and her feet rested on it. The unoccupied chair next to her seemed emptier than the one across from it, somehow. As Quinney watched, a girl came up to Marguerite and said, "Can I borrow this?"

Marguerite didn't answer her.

The girl cleared her throat and tried again. "Are you using this chair?"

"What does it look like?" Marguerite said, not even glancing her way. The girl shrugged, then dragged the chair off to an already-crowded table nearby.

Marguerite looked up—and saw Quinney watching her.

"Oh, hi," Quinney called out in a stagey voice. "I already finished eating—I was just clearing my tray."

It was an obvious lie, and she blushed saying it.

Marguerite stared at her, expressionless, but she didn't answer.

"Here I go," Quinney said as if she were narrating some lame documentary. "Here I go," she repeated to herself, and she headed toward the place where kids were supposed to dump their trash and return their dirty dishes to the kitchen through a steamy rectangular opening. With one scoop, Quinney's untasted lunch plopped onto a mound of garbage and she relinquished her tray.

So much for lunch, Quinney told herself as she turned her back on the cafeteria crowd—and on Marguerite.

CHAPTER TWENTY-ONE

People

"Quinney, help me dry this guy," Miss Mudge said later that afternoon, clasping the sheepdog-mix Mack had called Rags. "There are clean towels on the sofa over there—under Skinnybones." The long-legged gray cat leaped from the sofa as Quinney approached. She held Rags and tousled him gently with the rough towel.

Miss Mudge sniffed the air appreciatively. "Nothing like the aroma of a freshly washed dog."

"He smells like a wet sweater," Quinney said, wrinkling her nose. She dried the dog tenderly, though, and something that had been clenched inside her chest since lunchtime seemed to melt as she worked. Brynn was wrong, she thought—it wasn't that she wanted to control the animals at Whiskertown. It's just that they were so easy to love.

Rags threw his head back and tried to lick her face

upside down. "You goofball," Quinney said, laughing.

"That dog really likes you," Miss Mudge observed.

Quinney sighed. "I only wish that—*hey*," she said, as Rags grabbed the towel and started tugging on it. He made little grunting sounds as he pulled.

When toweled dry, Rags's hair stood up in enormous tufts. The dog reminded Quinney of Teddy and Mack after they'd taken showers.

Teddy and Mack. Quinney sighed again, thinking of Teddy playing alone with Jeremy this very afternoon, and Mack—stuck with Marguerite, if she'd even bothered to show up after school.

But Quinney didn't like thinking about Marguerite, not after what had happened at school.

Not noticing Quinney's expression, Miss Mudge put Rags in a freshly cleaned enclosure along with a dish of puppy chow and a bowl of water. From atop Miss Mudge's desk, Senator looked on, composed as always.

"Your flowers still look pretty, Miss Mudge," Quinney said shyly. Only the Queen Anne's lace was wilted, and Miss Mudge carefully plucked these drooping stalks out of the arrangement and threw them away.

"Thanks," the woman said. "Silly, really."

"Oh, I think it was nice of Dr. Havers," Quinney said.

Miss Mudge sniffed. "He's a good vet, I suppose. More than that I will not say."

◎

After most of the afternoon chores had been completed, Quinney and Miss Mudge perched on the red desk and shared triangles of peanut butter-and-jelly sandwiches that Miss Mudge had brought. Ravenous, Quinney wolfed down her share. Rags begged for scraps, but Miss Mudge told him, "Absolutely not. Don't be ridiculous. Can't you see we have a starving girl here?" She handed Quinney one of her own triangles.

"I'm not really starving," Quinney said through a mouthful of peanut butter, wishing she had a glass of cold milk to drink. "I just missed lunch, that's all." Her chest felt tight again when she remembered the scene with Marguerite in the cafeteria.

"That won't do," Miss Mudge said severely.

Quinney looked around Whiskertown suddenly, realizing that some animals were missing. "What happened to those puppies?" she asked, trying to change the subject and swallow a last bite of sandwich at the same time. "You know, the hunting dogs, sort of?"

"'Sort of' is right," Miss Mudge said, laughing. "David ended up taking them home with him. One of the pups started coughing right after you left on Saturday. At least she waited until after the opening."

"Oh, no!" Quinney exclaimed. "I hope they're all right. Rags isn't coughing, is he?"

"Listen for yourself—he's fine. And David called just after lunch today to say that the one pup's cough has almost cleared up and the other shows no sign of illness at all. He'll bring them back this weekend," she added, blushing a little. "Maybe he'll bring Shag, too."

"Shag?"

"His golden retriever," Miss Mudge told her. "But enough chitchat—time to get back to work."

Quinney hummed a little as she returned to work—flea-combing Senator, now. The big cat was limp, almost hypnotized, under her busy hands. After each stroke, Quinney dropped loose fur from the comb into a dish of heavily soaped water.

Finishing at last with his tail, she plopped him down next to her and reached for Skinnybones, who had been watching the combing procedure intently. Senator leaped up onto the top of a nearby enclosure and started scratching his neck as if Quinney had corralled several fleas there and instructed them to drive him wild.

Quinney and Miss Mudge laughed. "I still say it's worth combing them. We're not going to end up with *more* fleas, anyway," Miss Mudge said, settling into a creaky old desk chair, and Quinney continued to work on the ecstatic Skinnybones.

Miss Mudge arranged her long pleated skirt over her thin legs, opened a bill, and sighed. "It seems like a losing battle sometimes." She sounded discouraged.

"But it's not," Quinney said, trying to keep her boss's

spirits up. "Look at all the good you've done already."

Miss Mudge shrugged a bony shoulder and poked at some unopened bills. "Oh, I don't know," she said, clearly wanting Quinney to continue.

"Well, you have," Quinney stated, meaning it. She worked the comb along Skinnybones's elegant flank, and the cat stretched his leg out to help. "Look how happy *he* is, for instance," Quinney said, stroking the purring cat. Again, the invisible clench in her chest eased.

Miss Mudge nodded. "So," she asked, after a moment, "is your friend all right, now?"

"She's fine," Quinney said, sounding a little sour—and feeling guilty. "She moved in with us—into my bedroom. For who knows how long."

"That's too bad," Miss Mudge said, sounding sympathetic.

"Well," Quinney explained, "it's only supposed to be until her mom and dad pull themselves together."

"Why? What's wrong with her folks? I thought your friend was the one who had the accident."

"Yeah, but Mr. Harper is really having a problem with the whole thing. I guess some people at work were hassling him, and—"

"Oh, people," Miss Mudge interrupted, with what sounded like a snort. "Say no more. I know all about people, thank you very much, and what they're bound to say." She shoved the stack of bills into a neater pile.

"Marguerite *knew* those guys were going to be drinking, I think, but she got in the car with them anyway," Quinney said, trying to recapture some of her second-period anger. She worked the comb through Skinnybones's fur.

Miss Mudge remained silent.

"And not only that," Quinney added, pausing for a moment. "She doesn't even seem sorry. Not one little bit."

"And you want her to apologize? To beg your forgiveness?" Miss Mudge asked, tilting her head. She cradled her mug in her lap.

"Well, yeah," Quinney said. "I mean no, not beg. Not exactly. But she's not even sorry."

"You already said that," Miss Mudge observed. She stretched out her long legs and crossed her ankles.

"It's just that I'm worried about her," Quinney said, trying another approach—the mature approach, she thought, mentally gagging. "What if she gets in trouble eventually?"

"I thought she was already in trouble," Miss Mudge said, frowning.

"I meant—"

"Oh, you mean 'trouble.' As in pregnant," Miss Mudge said. "But you don't get pregnant from getting into cars with kids who've been drinking. Not right away, anyway."

"Yeah, but people—"

"There are those *people*, again," Miss Mudge exploded.

Skinnybones scrambled to his feet and streaked across the room.

"Let me tell you about *people*," Miss Mudge continued. "*People* believe what they want to believe. *People* talk about other people when their lives are so boring that they don't have anything else to do. And *people* talking is what almost ruined my life. So don't talk to me about *people*."

"They—they ruined your life?" Quinney asked, gaping.

"Almost," Miss Mudge corrected her, practically snapping out the word. "But don't worry, I was too tough for them."

"What happened?"

"Long story short," Miss Mudge said briskly. "Small town in Vermont, senior year in high school, had to go live with my aunt for a few months, rumor started that I was away somewhere having a baby, came back, life ruined. No one would talk to me—or my mother. *People*."

Quinney goggled at Miss Mudge, her head spinning. "But—but—but—" she sputtered.

"But?" Miss Mudge inquired with exaggerated politeness.

Quinney took a deep breath and began again. "But you didn't have a baby?"

"Nope," Miss Mudge said. "My mother was having emotional problems, and the family just thought it would be better if I went away for a while. That's not the point, though. The point is that people were all too happy to just go running off at the mouth, never thinking about me—or my poor mother," she finished, looking grim. "I got over the rumor, but she never did." Miss Mudge's shoulder went up in a tiny shrug.

"I—I'm sorry," Quinney said. She thought for a moment. "But there's a difference," she finally said.

"What's that?" Miss Mudge asked.

"Well, what happened to you was worse than what's happening to Marguerite because you didn't even do anything. You were innocent. And Marguerite—"

"What happened to me," Miss Mudge interrupted, "was that none of my so-called friends defended me or asked if they could help—not a one. That's what really hurt."

"But—so you're saying that I should stick up for Marguerite? Even though she was guilty?"

"Guilty of what?" Miss Mudge asked. "Bad judgment? And who's the judge—you? Let me ask you something," she said, shifting in her chair. "Were you friends with Marguerite because you thought she was perfect?"

"Well, no, of course not," Quinney said, irritated.

"So you're angry with her for what? Getting caught?"

"And for dragging me into it," Quinney blurted out. "You don't know what it's been like for me at school. It's so embarrassing!"

"Well, I'm sorry about that," Miss Mudge said, straightening her Whiskertown T-shirt. "But does that mean you'll never be able to forgive her?"

"Do you expect me to forgive someone when she isn't even sorry?" Quinney said.

This was so unfair!

"That's up to you," Miss Mudge replied, shrugging again. "It would be hard, I know."

"What about you?" Quinney asked, flushing angrily. "What if someone hurt a puppy or a kitten on purpose, just to be cruel? Would you forgive that person?"

"No way," Miss Mudge said flatly.

"What about if that person apologized?" Quinney continued, relentless.

"It would be hard," Miss Mudge admitted. "But if I didn't forgive whoever it was, that doesn't mean I'd be right. If he or she had hurt the animal by accident, though. . . ."

"Huh," Quinney said. "What Marguerite did was not exactly an accident." Sure, it had been understandable in a way, Quinney thought, remembering her tell-the-truth conversation with Marguerite, but that didn't make it right.

"Yes," Miss Mudge said slowly, "but involving you was an accident. And I'll bet she's sorry for that."

Quinney tried to remember. Marguerite *had* seemed upset when Quinney told her what those seventh-grade boys had said in the cafeteria. "Well, maybe," she said reluctantly.

"But if you can't forgive her, then you might as well just walk away right now," Miss Mudge said. "Do her a favor." Senator jumped onto her lap, and Miss Mudge began scratching his ears.

"I can't walk away," Quinney wailed. "She's living in my bedroom."

"You know what I mean," Miss Mudge said severely. "You should make up your mind, and soon—because your friend needs you now, and she needs to know if she flat-out can't count on you anymore. You're obviously not helping her any the way things stand."

Quinney blushed, remembering her disastrous day with Marguerite. She grumbled, "But I'm tired of helping her. It never ends. She's too high maintenance," she added, repeating a description she'd heard her mom use about a difficult, demanding woman she'd once worked with at the nursery school.

"Well, it will all even out," Miss Mudge told her. "And you might be the one who needs a little extra care and attention someday—just like these animals, here," she added fondly, looking around.

"Huh," Quinney said. "I guess it's a lot easier taking care of animals than it is taking care of people."

"You don't have to take care of your friends, Quinney—you just need to love them."

CHAPTER TWENTY-TWO

Outside the Blue Line

"**M**iss Mudge says I need to love you," Quinney told Marguerite that night after dinner. She was lying atop her fluffy chenille bedspread, flat on her back, untouched homework spread in drifts around her.

It had been an extremely awkward evening.

She was trying to keep her voice neutral. Neither of the two girls had mentioned Marguerite's first day back at school—or Quinney's betrayals, both during second period and in the school cafeteria.

"I knew she was gay," Marguerite snapped, not looking up from her magazine. She flicked a shiny page over and cracked the gum she was chewing.

Quinney scowled. "Well, she's not gay, as a matter of fact. She even has a boyfriend."

"I don't believe you," Marguerite said, and she yawned—without bothering to cover her mouth.

Quinney could see pale green chewing gum nestled in

the curve of her tongue. "Oh, that's nice," she remarked. "It looks like you've been eating a caterpillar."

"I might try eating caterpillars someday," Marguerite replied, shrugging. "Maybe soon—they couldn't be any worse than what we had for dinner tonight." She resumed her chewing. *Crick, crack.*

Angry, Quinney chewed her lower lip. The meat loaf her mother had thrown together at the last minute had tasted a little weird. Too many bread crumbs; she'd probably gotten distracted by the twins while making it. And then Marguerite picked a large tissuelike flake of onion skin that had somehow made it into the mixture and placed it on the edge of her plate with elaborate care—making sure only Quinney saw her.

"You never complained about my mom's cooking before," Quinney said.

Marguerite glanced over the top of her magazine at Quinney. "Well, tastes mature."

The nerve of her, Quinney thought, furious once more—always so ready to take credit for something that was nothing to be proud of! To hear Marguerite tell it, wearing too much makeup was creative, not cheap; jumping into a car with a bunch of high school boys was bold, not stupid; a taste for Quinney's mom's cooking was something to be outgrown.

"That's right," Quinney said, sitting up so suddenly that she felt dizzy for a moment. "Tastes do mature,

Marguerite—and that's why I think I've outgrown *you.*"

"Hah—that's a laugh," Marguerite said, not laughing at all. "If anything, it's the other way around."

Quinney looked up at the ceiling, as if thinking hard. "No," she finally said. "I've outgrown you. Brynn has, too."

"Oh, *Brynn,*" Marguerite scoffed. "Brynn's a dope." She flipped her magazine shut and tossed it to the foot of her bed, where it slid off and fell onto the floor.

"She is not a dope," Quinney said.

"Is too."

"Oh, that's real mature," Quinney shot back. "What are you going to do next, say 'neener-neener-neener'?"

Marguerite didn't answer. She reached over to the bedside table for her nail file.

"I refuse to keep choking on your nasty fingernail dust," Quinney exclaimed, exasperated. "If you file your nails in here one more time, Marguerite, why, I'm going to—I'm going to—"

"You're going to *what?*" Marguerite asked. "You're going to punch your teddy bear? Or hold your breath until you turn blue? Or stomp your tiny foot? Or walk out of the room while everyone is watching and pretend you don't even see me? Or tell your mommy and daddy?"

"At least my parents are talking to me. At least they can stand me," Quinney replied, furious at the pretend-you-don't-even-see-me remark.

It struck a little too close to home.

Marguerite jerked back as if Quinney had struck her, and Quinney saw the pain in the other girl's eyes. "Ooh, good one, Quinney," she said, and then—as if miniblinds had suddenly been twisted shut—her hurt expression vanished.

"I'm sorry, Marguerite," Quinney whispered, feeling terrible. "I shouldn't have said that."

Marguerite shrugged a shoulder still tan from summer hours spent lying on Lake Geneva's scrubby shore. "Say what you like. Only I don't see why you have to talk so much at home when you won't give me the time of day at school." She looked down, examining her toenails.

There it was again. "Well," Quinney blustered, "what about when you were rude to me at Whiskertown, you and your brand-new friends? And then acting nice in front of my mom. You faker."

"You're the faker," Marguerite said. "You're just so totally nice to everyone all the time, aren't you? Everyone else, I mean, the people who don't really need you. You're so totally sweet. Everyone's favorite girl," she finished, a sneer distorting her face.

"Not your favorite, apparently," Quinney said, trying to make her voice sound bored.

"Not anymore," Marguerite said softly. "Not anymore." "Well," she added in a voice that was almost natural, "I don't want to keep on embarrassing you. I'm leaving the Todd residence, as of now." She stood up.

"You can't go," Quinney said. "We're stuck here together. Anyway, where would you go?"

"Outside the blue line," Marguerite said, referring to the drawn boundary that outlined the huge Adirondack Park on all regional maps. Lake Geneva was just inside the boundary. "I always told you I was going to blow this Popsicle stand, didn't I?"

"But where would you go? Vermont? Albany? Canada? You're lying."

Marguerite shrugged again and dumped her school backpack onto the bed. Books and binders tumbled everywhere. She started opening drawers; she pulled out underpants, bras, and T-shirts and jammed them into the empty backpack with a ferocity that alarmed Quinney.

"You're lying," Quinney repeated, trying to convince herself. "You're not going anywhere—it's dark out. It's after ten o'clock."

"Just watch me." Marguerite shoved her arms into her black denim jacket, hoisted her backpack over one shoulder, then headed down the stairs, silent.

Quinney grabbed a sweater, pulled on shoes, and followed. She didn't want to yell for her parents; Marguerite would get into even more trouble, and besides, she knew that this latest blowup was her fault, really.

If her parents knew how she'd behaved, she'd be in trouble. Big trouble. She should be the one to straighten things out. To calm Marguerite down.

"Marguerite," she whispered urgently as Marguerite went out the kitchen door. "Come back—let's talk."

Marguerite waited until she'd reached the street to answer, and even then her soft words seemed almost to melt in the damp night air. "Leave me alone. There's nothing to talk about."

"But I'm sorry!" Quinney said, forgetting to be quiet.

"It's too late for sorry."

One lone road—9N—connected the town of Lake Geneva with the rest of the world. If you followed it out the south end of town, it led to Marathon, home of the paper mill that employed so many local people.

Just past the north end of Lake Geneva, though, the road curved east, and from that point on it was seven long, empty miles through forests, until you reached the Northway. Beyond the turnoff for the Northway were the northernmost outskirts of the city of Peters Falls.

Quinney had been driven those seven miles so many times in her life that it was impossible to count them, but she had never once walked this road in the daytime—let alone at night.

Quinney trudged after Marguerite. "Come back," she called. "Let's talk." The few lights illuminating the road grew farther and farther apart; Quinney tripped over a rotten branch that had collapsed onto the road, and she muttered a few choice words under her steaming breath.

Walking along this road wasn't even safe during the daytime, not really, she thought, a flush of indignation and worry warming her body as Marguerite stalked on ahead. Cars and trucks often sped along the curvy road, despite the frequent accidents that smashed up their sometimes-boozy occupants.

It was not a road meant for pedestrians.

"Marguerite," Quinney yelled again. She clutched her sweater tighter around her, hoping that it hid her pajamas.

Without turning around, Marguerite shouted something in return, but her reply was grabbed by the wind like a tiny scrap of tissue paper. Quinney didn't know what she'd said.

Marguerite was obviously headed out of town. Was she going to walk all the way to Peters Falls? Or was she simply walking? Moving one leg after the other, with no clear destination in mind?

Leaves swirled and twirled crazily though the night air. If you could stop time for a second, Quinney thought dully, the sky might look almost polka-dotted.

Marguerite looked like a Barbie doll from far away, with her tight Levis, snug jacket, and chunky platform shoes. Quinney paused to shake a small stone from her own shoe. I could catch up to her in a minute if I ran, she thought. But then what? I can't *drag* her back. She watched as Marguerite stumbled, and she hurried to catch up in spite of her misgivings.

"Hey, wait," she called out. "I'm really sorry I said those things. I'm sorry about school, too. I just panicked. You can't go!"

"I don't have a choice," Marguerite yelled over her shoulder. "You don't want me, and my parents don't want me either."

"They call you all the time, don't they?" What was Marguerite talking about? Oh, sure, Mr. and Mrs. Harper were acting sort of goofy. They reminded Quinney of cuckoo-clock people, whirling around in a useless circle every time the hour struck. But they would pull themselves together soon, wouldn't they?

In spite of her clunky shoes, Marguerite was picking up speed. "It's late—come on home," Quinney called out. She started to trot, trying to catch up, but then a car whizzed by through the darkness and she slowed down, feeling foolish.

Marguerite shouted out some words that Quinney couldn't hear.

The girls passed a campground, almost deserted this cold September night; the few die-hard campers who had lingered past the end of the summer season were all asleep. "Wait up!" Quinney called. She started running again.

Things happened fast after that.

Marguerite looked back, and at the same time both girls heard a truck approaching. Marguerite wrenched her face into a smile aimed at the truck and stuck out her thumb to hitch a ride.

"Marguerite, *no!*" Quinney cried.

"I told you—I have to live outside the line," Marguerite yelled back, and she jerked her thumb in the air again. An old red pickup rolled to a halt in front of them, a *thump-thump* of loud music pouring from its open windows.

The driver stuck his head out of the window, and another man opened the passenger door. They looked as if they were in their thirties, Quinney thought; the driver had long hair pulled back into a ponytail, and a stained, faded rodeo T-shirt peeked through his black-and-white plaid flannel jacket. His equally scruffy passenger obviously hadn't shaved in days. Quinney didn't recognize either of them, but that wasn't unusual. Lots of people—drifters, guys hunting illegally—made their way through this relatively crowded part of the Adirondacks.

"Well, hey," the driver cried out, grinning. He banged the side of his truck three times with his fist as if he'd just gotten some good news.

Quinney had finally caught up to Marguerite. "Don't do it," she said, keeping an eye on the men in the truck.

"I have to," Marguerite answered softly. "There's nothing for me here, Quinney. Nobody at school is going to let me forget what happened. No one's going to give me a second chance."

"Come on—ain't got all day, do we?" the driver almost

howled into the cold night air.

"Whoo-eee!" the passenger-side man shouted, like a bad guy in a TV show. Marguerite took a step in his direction.

A dozen images flooded Quinney's mind. She saw Marguerite, Brynn, and herself swinging clasped hands back and forth like pistons as they walked along the corrugated dirt ruts of River Road—late in May, just before their final weeks of elementary school.

She saw a six-year-old Marguerite who hadn't been invited to a much-talked-about birthday party; Quinney and Brynn, although asked, had opted to stay home with their friend, and Quinney's mom had made them an unbirthday cake.

She saw herself as a ten-year-old, in Lake Geneva's market—the town's one place to buy groceries—bumping into Marguerite, who was about to make a doomed attempt at shoplifting—practically under the nose of fierce Mrs. Bloom, the head checkout lady, too—although Marguerite didn't realize that, of course. "Thanks for finding those for me," Quinney had said loudly, grabbing the package of Reese's Peanut Butter Cups just before Marguerite slipped them into her sweatshirt pouch. Quinney tossed the candy into her grocery cart and paid her mom back for them from her own allowance. Marguerite thanked her, but neither of them had felt much like eating the candy. They'd given it to the twins.

She saw her hand slicing through tea-colored lake

water, reaching to pull Marguerite to her feet.

But sometimes, it was Marguerite's hand that seemed to reach across dark water to pull Quinney to safety. Wasn't it Marguerite who had pretended to faint in the fourth grade that time, just to save Quinney—who was about to get in serious trouble for her hysterical giggle attack when their teacher said, "Let's keep abreast, people"?

Wasn't it Marguerite who had found a ten-year-old Quinney crying silently in the drugstore behind the flip-flop display, too embarrassed to buy the box of Tampax her mom needed? Didn't Marguerite march right up to the cashier and buy the box herself, not even bothering to hide the label? And there had been boys around, too.

They were friends because—because they were friends. And in that instant, Quinney realized that she loved her friend the same way she loved her parents and little brothers—and Rags, too, for that matter.

She loved them without even thinking about it.

She saw her friend silhouetted in the truck's fuzzy red taillights. Marguerite seemed to be suspended midstep; her hair seemed electric, curly from the damp, and haloed. "Wait," Quinney cried out. "If you really want a second chance, I'll give you one. I promise."

Marguerite turned slowly to face Quinney, looking as though she wanted to believe her. Then she shook her head slowly. "No," she said. "I hurt you enough already."

So, Quinney thought, Marguerite *did* realize what

she'd done to the people around her. That meant a lot.

"Admit it for once, Quinney—you hate having me live with you," Marguerite said. "You're embarrassed!"

"Yeah," Quinney admitted. "But—but now I want you to stay." She was surprised to discover that she meant what she was saying. She glanced nervously at the truck. The guy on the passenger side had gotten out now and was staring at them as if they were two deer caught in the headlights. "You're like my sister," Quinney said urgently.

"But we fight," Marguerite said. "I don't want to be just another stray animal to you, Quinney—one of your charities."

"Real sisters fight, don't they? We'll just have to get used to it, I guess."

"Come *on!*" the driver hollered. The passenger-side man took a step toward Marguerite. His greasy hair gleamed in the moonlight.

Marguerite looked at Quinney, her face as blank as a newly erased blackboard. She shook her head. "I'm going," she said.

"Then—then I'm going, too," Quinney announced, astonished at her own words. If Marguerite would be even a little bit safer with her in the truck, then she'd get in the stupid truck!

But her heart was beating so hard that she didn't know whether she was about to pass out or be sick, right there in the road.

186

"You can't come," Marguerite said. "You have a family."

"Well, you do, too. Your mom and dad love you a lot. And I'm your family, too. I'm your oldest friend. I'm your sister. Sister Quinney."

And the truth of what she was saying was as clear as water to Quinney at that moment: You could choose your own family as you got older. Why not? What Brynnie had said—that everything changes—was true. But this was true, too, Quinney knew. Different things could be true at the same time.

"All *right*," the ponytailed driver yelled with fierce enthusiasm. "It's a two-for-one deal! There's room for everyone."

"She changed her mind," Quinney shouted back, grabbing Marguerite's cold hand. "We both did."

The two men exchanged furious glances, and then the passenger-side man shrugged and laughed a little. "Too good to be true," he said, climbing back into the truck.

The driver, though, was angry. His spit hit the ground as if meant for Quinney and Marguerite, then he revved the engine and pulled away, his wheels hurling roadside gravel into the air.

"I think we were just very, very lucky," Quinney told her friend in a shaky voice.

"Oh, well," Marguerite said lightly. "There will always be another truck, I guess—if I ever need it." But Quinney was pretty sure Marguerite didn't mean what she'd just said; she could feel her friend's hand still trembling. "Would you really have gotten into that truck if I did?" Marguerite asked.

"Yes," Quinney answered.

"Then you would have been extremely stupid," Marguerite said, as if stating an obvious fact. "Even stupider than I was to get into the car with those high school boys that afternoon."

"Maybe," Quinney said. "I guess you have to decide for yourself how stupid you're going to be—and then you have to figure it out brand-new every day."

"But—but what if other people won't let you be the one to decide—or to change, even?" Marguerite asked. She was obviously thinking of the kids at school—the older boys who had bothered Quinney, but also of girls like Erika, and Carla, and maybe even Brynnie, her onetime friend. And Quinney, at least up until half an hour ago.

"Oh, *people*," Quinney said, shaking her head. "You fight back. You find new people." They turned around and started the long walk home.

"Huh," Marguerite said, pleased. She straightened her jacket. "So, what are you going to say if your mom and dad are awake when we get back?" she asked after a moment, tilting her head.

"Let me think," Quinney said, fervently hoping they were fast asleep. "Should I tell them that we decided to go bowling? That there was a field trip we forgot to tell them about? That we just wanted to get a little exercise? And then they'll say something, and then I'll say something, and . . ."

Marguerite laughed. "This I gotta hear."

"Well, you will," Quinney told her. "All night long, if they really are awake."

"Hey," Marguerite said. "At least they care. It doesn't sound so bad to me."

Actually, it sounded pretty good to Quinney, too.

CHAPTER TWENTY-THREE
A Little Bit Right

The Todds were up, and the girls were grounded for two weeks, except for Marguerite's two family counseling sessions and Quinney's obligations at the library and Whiskertown. "They did come right back," Mrs. Todd pointed out to her husband, who'd been in favor of a much harsher punishment. "It was just a stupid whim, taking a nighttime stroll like that."

Quinney and Marguerite hadn't told Quinney's parents about the men in the old red truck; that was their secret.

At home, they either hung out together or avoided each other—like real sisters. They weren't allowed to watch TV or make phone calls, so Quinney got a lot of reading done. Marguerite daydreamed and played with the twins.

Marguerite came home from her counseling sessions in Peters Falls sometimes moody, sometimes elated. Quinney was curious about the sessions, but Marguerite told her she didn't want to talk about it.

The days passed.

Two weeks later it was almost time for Marguerite to go home; the Todds were getting ready to give a farewell picnic Sunday afternoon.

Even though their guests were bringing food to share, Marguerite and the Todd family cooked for the entire weekend. On Saturday they made three batches of cookies and a pan of brownies. "These will keep for a while," Quinney's mom said. "Especially if we hide them," she added, sneaking a look at her husband.

He glanced up from the big wooden spoon he was licking clean. "Hmm?" he said dreamily, and Quinney and Marguerite burst into laughter.

Next, Quinney's father made five loaves of bread. Mrs. Todd took a nap; she was taking naps whenever she could lately, Quinney had noticed. The fragrance of the baking loaves drove everyone who was awake wild. "I don't think I can wait," Mack moaned.

Saturday evening Quinney's dad drove the boys into Peters Falls to pick up paper plates, cups, napkins, and tablecloths for the picnic. "Don't forget," Mrs. Todd said. "We're borrowing that second picnic table, so we'll need two big tablecloths. And extra plates for dessert."

"Yeah—since we're having at least three desserts," Marguerite said, laughing.

While they were gone, Quinney and Marguerite boiled eggs for deviled eggs and for the potato salad. After they finished, they shredded two heads of cabbage for coleslaw. "We'll toss it at the last minute," Mrs. Todd told them.

"I hope everybody will be good and hungry," Marguerite said, popping half a deviled egg into her mouth.

"Yeah—but we might have to send them to that McDonald's in Peters Falls for dinner if we keep snacking like this," Quinney said, helping herself to the other half of the egg.

"I don't know," Quinney said fretfully the Sunday afternoon of the picnic. She eased up the zipper of a faded sundress. "How does this look?" She turned to face her friend, who was sitting cross-legged on the bed.

"Kinda tight, but that's good," Marguerite said, narrowing her eyes. "Who would have thought you could be wearing a sleeveless dress the last weekend in September?" She clambered to her feet and stood next to Quinney in front of the full-length mirror on Quinney's closet door.

Quinney looked a little older than she had when September began, she thought, and Marguerite looked a bit younger. Quinney's hair was shorter now. At Marguerite's suggestion, she'd had it cut the other day so it swung just above her shoulders. There was a touch of color on her lips. "'Crushed Raspberry Glaze,'" Marguerite had said, reading the tiny print at the bottom of the lipstick.

Quinney pressed her lips together. "Don't eat it all off," Marguerite scolded.

Marguerite's own face was free of makeup at the moment, and Quinney thought her friend had never looked prettier. She was dressed simply, wearing her faded black Levis and the new white T-shirt Mrs. Harper had bought her, just snug enough. The stitches above her eye were long gone and the bruises faded. Marguerite's wide-set light brown eyes looked almost golden in the light that streamed in the room's two windows. Her long brown hair was tangled, but shining clean.

"You look good that way," Quinney said, staring at Marguerite in the mirror.

"What way?" Marguerite ruffled her bangs self-consciously.

"You know, simple."

"Oh," Marguerite said, looking pleased. "Well, you look good, too. Complicated."

Quinney fluffed her hair away from her neck and resisted the urge to press her lips together again. "Complicated is okay," she said, still looking in the mirror. "You know, Marguerite, you shouldn't leave here if you're not ready to."

Marguerite gave a tiny shrug and returned to her bed. "I guess I'm as ready as I'll ever be."

"But maybe that's not good enough."

"It's gotta be," Marguerite said.

Quinney shook her head. "Is that the counselor talking, or is that you talking?" she asked.

"She doesn't put words in my mouth," Marguerite said. "And I'm still just as messed up as ever, so don't worry, Quinney. Gee, I thought you'd be dying to get rid of me by now," she added, joking—a little.

Quinney thought about the last two weeks. There had been squabbles over little things, such as who would get to shower first, or who had to get up to turn off the overhead light at night after they'd finished reading.

There had been bigger fights, too. One day after school, Marguerite spent the better part of an hour telling Quinney exactly what was wrong with the Todds. "You guys are exactly like those stupid little rugs," she said as she pointed scornfully at the braided rugs on Quinney's bedroom floor. "You're just so old-fashioned," she added, in case Quinney missed her point—which she hadn't.

The nerve of Marguerite.

But still, Quinney thought, if she had to be a floor covering, she'd rather be a lovingly crafted rag rug than the finest, cushiest wall-to-wall carpeting in the world. "Oh, I am dying to get rid of you, *believe* me," she told Marguerite, grinning. "Just think, I'll be able to see my floor again." She looked down at the piles of Marguerite's T-shirts and nightgowns that were scattered around the room.

"It was for your own good that I always made a mess," Marguerite said. "And admit it—I've been good for you. You're a lot looser now."

"That's not loose, that's nervous," Quinney said, flapping her arms helplessly in the air.

But Marguerite was a little bit right, she admitted to herself—because hadn't she picked up the phone just yesterday and called Cree Scovall? She never would have done *that* before—not just to talk. It was only to tell him about the picnic, of course—and to invite him, although she and Cree had ultimately decided that it might be a little weird if he came. It might make Marguerite feel funny, and the party was in her honor. But he promised to call her to find out how it went.

"So, who else is coming?" Marguerite asked, as if somehow sensing Quinney's thoughts.

"Oh, let's see," Quinney said, tapping her chin and gazing up at the ceiling. "Besides your mom and dad, there's Miss Mudge and Dr. Havers, and Mrs. Arbuckle-the-librarian, and Jeremy, for the twins. All three of them are friends, now. Oh," she added. "And Jeremy's parents are coming, and Brynnie's coming, and Brynn's mom, and Sam. I invited Charlotte, but her mother won't let her anywhere near me—or Whiskertown, for that matter. But Brynnie and Charlotte are such great friends, now," she added, making a little face.

"Jealous?" Marguerite asked. "Tell the truth."

"Okay," Quinney said reluctantly. "*Kind of,* but I'm also a little glad for Charlotte, because her parents are so weird. Apart from helping her save Marshmallow, I haven't been such a good friend to her—not that her mother's made it any easier. Now, you tell the truth. Are you scared to go home?"

"*Kind of,*" Marguerite echoed, "but only because *my* parents are so weird."

The girls looked at each other and burst out laughing. "Oh, stop," Quinney begged. "I think I'm about to break the zipper on this stupid dress."

"Camera! Where's a camera when you really need one?" Marguerite called out, pretending to search.

"You wouldn't dare." The faded dress suddenly gaped opened at the side seam with an audible *pop.*

The girls stared down at the crescent of exposed flesh, silent for a moment. "Hmm. Maybe I should really loosen up and get a big old tattoo," Quinney said thoughtfully—which was when they both started to howl with laughter.

Instantly, the twins were at the door. "What's going on in there?" Mack yelled, knocking as hard as he could. "Are you guys socking each other?"

It was only on her way downstairs, after she'd changed into faded Levis, a black T-shirt, and flip-flops, that Quinney remembered Monty, the twins's imaginary friend. Where had he been lately? It was as though the twins had been so busy starting kindergarten and having Marguerite around that they'd forgotten all about him. So had she.

Monty hadn't even gone with them up to Bear Slide, Quinney realized.

Poor Monty.

"Jeez, Quinney—you look like you're about to cry," Marguerite said, getting a soda from the refrigerator. "You're going to wreck your face."

"It's just the onions," Quinney said, sniffling a little.

Marguerite peered around the crowded countertops and looked as though she was about to say, "What onions?" But instead, she gave Quinney a little hug.

The weather was perfect. Almost everything was ready; Quinney and Marguerite had helped Mrs. Todd make hamburger patties, and turkey sausages and a big baked ham sat waiting in the refrigerator. So did the sliced vegetables, ready for grilling. "I don't think anyone will starve," Quinney's mother finally said, and the three of them washed their hands in the old kitchen sink.

Looking out the back window, Quinney saw that Teddy and Mack were struggling to move the two large folding picnic tables. Mr. Todd had dragged them out of the garage early that morning and leaned them against the thick, double-trunked birch tree in their backyard.

197

Quinney's dad appeared and began helping the boys set up the tables and chairs. From where Quinney stood, father and sons seemed to present a pantomime of misunderstood directions and hurt feelings. Soon, however, everything was in place. "Put some rocks on the table-cloths," Mrs. Todd told the boys, "and come on inside—it's time to get dressed for the picnic." She always saved dressing the twins for the last minute. That way, there was at least a sporting chance that they'd look presentable when guests arrived.

The twins were so excited that they didn't even complain about changing their clothes. They climbed dutifully into clean shorts and pulled fresh T-shirts over their heads. They could tie their own sneakers now, but Quinney and Marguerite helped them brush their hair.

"Part my hair in the middle," Mack instructed Quinney. "I want people to be able to tell the difference between me and Teddy."

"Yeah," Teddy agreed. The two boys looked at one another, pleased with this new idea.

Oh, great, Quinney thought. Now one of her little brothers looked like an escapee from a barbershop quartet.

Jeremy and his mom and dad—who Quinney thought of as Mr. and Mrs. Jeremy—were the first guests to arrive. Mrs. Jeremy handed Quinney's mom a big bowl and said, "It's a cold Chinese noodle dish."

"What's that?" Teddy whispered to Jeremy, while Mack glared with suspicion at the covered bowl.

"It's what cold Chinese people eat," Jeremy whispered back. All three boys grinned at each other, delighted.

Mrs. Arbuckle arrived next. "I brought some fruit," she said, embarrassed at being the temporary center of attention but proud of her accomplishment.

"Oh, girls, look at this," Quinney's mother said admiringly. The librarian had cut a watermelon to resemble a big scalloped basket. Inside the basket were perfect little balls of watermelon and cantaloupe mixed with strawberries, blueberries, and chunks of fresh pineapple.

"It's so pretty," Quinney said.

"Yeah," Marguerite agreed, flicking a polite glance at the fruit basket.

"Oh, excuse me—this is Marguerite Harper, Mrs. Arbuckle," Quinney's mom said, making the introduction.

"Hello," Mrs. Arbuckle said. She seemed to have heard of Marguerite, even though Marguerite had not spent a lot of time in the library.

While Quinney was busy in the kitchen fixing Mrs. Arbuckle and all the Jeremys tall icy glasses of lemonade, Brynn, Mrs. Mathers, and Sam Weir arrived at the party. By the time Quinney carried the drink-laden tray into the yard, Brynnie was deep in conversation with Marguerite under the birch tree.

So that was going to be okay—at least for today,

Quinney thought. Feeling a little awkward, she joined them. "Hey, Brynnie."

"Hey."

Marguerite smoothed back a wing of brown hair with a seemingly careless gesture.

"You can't even tell you were in an accident," Brynn told her. "Did—did it hurt a lot?"

"Nah—hardly at all," Marguerite said, nonchalant. "I can barely remember a thing about it."

"Marguerite, honey," Mrs. Todd said gently, looming up suddenly in the gathering dusk. "Your parents are here—in the living room. Want to come say hello?"

Mr. Harper was wearing a brown-and-white patterned shirt that hung loose over his brand-new blue Levis. Standing next to the empty sofa, he and his wife looked lost, as though they were wondering where the party was. Mr. Harper shifted uneasily from foot to foot as Marguerite, Quinney, and Brynn trooped into the room. Marguerite had insisted that they come with her. "Hey, baby," he greeted Marguerite.

"Honey," Mrs. Harper said. "You look so nice." The three Harpers embraced awkwardly, out of practice.

Next to Quinney, Brynn sighed.

"Everyone's in the backyard," Marguerite told her parents, voice muffled.

"Anita, Frank, can Quinney get you something to

drink?" Quinney's mom asked Mr. and Mrs. Harper. "We have lemonade, soda, beer . . ."

"I'll have a diet soda," Mrs. Harper said.

"I'll take a—a large lemonade," Mr. Harper said.

Quinney realized it was the first time she would see Mr. Harper drink something other than beer.

Marguerite smiled.

CHAPTER TWENTY-FOUR

Surprise!

Miss Mudge and David-the-Vet were the last guests to arrive at the Todds' picnic. From the kitchen window, rinsing an extra batch of cherry tomatoes in a battered mesh colander to replace the ones the twins had just spilled, Quinney saw a shiny black four-by-four pull up in the driveway. She ran outside to greet them.

David-the-Vet stepped from the driver's seat. He lifted a hand in solemn greeting, but he also gave Quinney the broadest smile she had ever seen. He was wearing khaki pants, a white shirt with rolled-up sleeves, and a navy blue bow tie with white polka dots.

Quinney thought he looked very nice. She was glad he'd gotten dressed up for their party—after all, it was a special occasion.

Marguerite was going to rejoin her family.

Miss Mudge hurried around the front of the car, her hair falling from its bun. "Sorry we're late," she said, jabbing a shimmery chopstick back in place. "But we had to go pick something up."

"That's okay," Quinney said. "There's still plenty of food left, and Dad's just started cooking the meat."

Miss Mudge brushed animal hair from her Whiskertown T-shirt—a brand-new one, Quinney noticed, so pristine that it still had its creases—and smoothed her long skirt.

Dr. Havers opened a back door of the car and brought out a large sealed plastic bag. "It's peanut brittle," he said.

Miss Mudge snorted. "It's *homemade* peanut brittle," she said. "David did everything himself but grow the darn peanuts."

"Thanks," Quinney said, taking the bag from him.

"Wait until you see what *I* brought to eat, Quinney," Miss Mudge said. "It's in a huge sack in the back."

Quinney peered into the truck's dark-tinted windows and saw a big furry head bobbing back and forth excitedly. "Oh, you brought Shag with you," she said, thrilled.

"Well, of course we brought Shag," Miss Mudge said. "He was invited, wasn't he?

"Oh, sure," Quinney said hurriedly. "Wait until the twins see him—they'll be so excited."

Dr. Havers swung open the tailgate. A beautiful animal leaped out of the truck and onto the driveway. "Sit," Dr. Havers told his dog quietly, and he sat. Quinney almost did, too, so authoritative was his command.

"Let me get that sack before we go in," Miss Mudge said, and she hauled out what looked like—what looked like a giant bag of kibble, Quinney realized. Twenty-five pounds of it.

She laughed. "I see you brought his dinner."

"He's already eaten," Dr. Havers said, his eyes shining with amusement.

"Then what—*ohhh*," Quinney said.

Because Miss Mudge was now hauling out a second bundle. Rags! "Come on, doofus," she said to the extraordinarily fluffy young dog. "Did that big old golden scare you silly?" She snapped a brand-new red leather leash to the dog's collar and lifted him onto the grass.

"Oh, Miss Mudge," Quinney said with a gasp. "You brought Rags to the picnic, too!"

"Is he here yet? Is he here?" Mr. Todd said, barreling through the kitchen door.

"Is who here?" Mack asked. Teddy and Jeremy followed close behind, curious.

Rags spotted Mr. Todd and the boys and bounded over to them, tail thrashing. He yelped with joy. "Don't let him jump," Miss Mudge warned, but it was too late—Rags, Mr. Todd, Teddy, Mack, and Jeremy were all leaping around with excitement. Miss Mudge's arm, holding on to the leash, jumped up and down, too.

Mrs. Todd appeared at the kitchen door, and a big smile spread across her face when she saw what was going on. "Were you surprised?" she called out.

Quinney was so flabbergasted she could barely speak. "But—but—but—"

Mr. Todd broke free of the dog-and-boy melee. He slapped her on the back as if helping her to clear her throat. "We did it," he crowed, shooting his wife a triumphant look. "We actually put something over on our Miss Quinney!"

"But—but—"

"She's stuck, Norm," Mrs. Todd said, rushing over to hug her daughter. "There you go," she soothed.

"But—but I thought you guys didn't want to ever get another dog," Quinney finally managed to say. "I believed you! So I wasn't even trying to get you to adopt Rags, even though I—"

"Well, we just figured 'What the heck,' right, Marge?" Quinney's dad interrupted. "We thought that as long as there's going to be another—"

"Norm," Mrs. Todd said quietly. "Now might not be the best time—"

"For what?" Quinney demanded. "You mean there's *more*?"

Quinney's parents looked at each other solemnly for a moment, and then they couldn't help it—they started to laugh. Mrs. Todd fell into her husband's arms. "Oh, Norman," she said, starting to cry a little.

"Mom," Quinney said, alarmed. "Are you all right?"

"She's fine, honey," Mr. Todd said, reaching out his arm to gather Quinney into their embrace. "She's just going to have a baby, that's all."

Maybe-baby.

"Surprise!" Mrs. Todd said, her tear-streaked cheeks creasing in an amazing smile.

"This reminds me of something funny Mark Twain once said about new babies," Mr. Todd said, suppressing a laugh. "It seems there was this—"

"Norman," his wife interrupted fondly, "now *really* may not be the best time."

Mack trotted up holding the end of Rags's leash while Teddy and Jeremy hung on to the middle. "Can we keep him?" Mack asked.

"Sure, we can keep him," Mr. Todd said. "We're all ready for him."

"And you folks had better take good care of him, too," Miss Mudge broke in. "Or we're all moving in with you to supervise, the whole mob of us. Your new dog run is in my storage area—it starts going up tomorrow."

"We've got a dog run," Teddy told Jeremy, amazed.

"Oh, Rags," Quinney said, kneeling next to the puppy and burying her face in his fur. She tried not to worry about the new baby for the time being; it was enough to be happy right now. She looked up and smiled at everyone. "He smells so good."

"Of course he does. David just gave him a bubble bath," Miss Mudge said.

After dinner everyone sat back on the blankets Quinney's dad had spread out on cool grass, and Quinney and Marguerite lit candles and arranged them along the picnic tables.

"Miss Smudge," Teddy asked drowsily. "How did Rags get his name, anyway?"

"Your brother named him, dear," Miss Mudge said, passing Mrs. Arbuckle some more peanut brittle. The two women had really hit it off; it looked as though they might even become friends.

"I named him," Mack confirmed, nodding importantly.

"But how did Mack get the idea?" Teddy persisted.

Miss Mudge caught Quinney's eye, and they laughed. Both of them remembered Miss Mudge crying, "*Quinney, Rags!*" each time the puppy made a puddle on the floor at Whiskertown.

"Your sister will tell you," Miss Mudge answered.

"Not tonight, though," Quinney said. "Besides, I'm afraid you'll find out soon enough."

"Let's just say that a dog needs a lot of love and attention," Miss Mudge said instructively. "It's not a toy. You can't ignore it if you get bored with it—it won't go away."

Babies won't, either, Quinney thought in spite of herself.

"We won't get bored. We'll give it attention," the twins chorused.

"And walks. Dogs have to have walks every day, you know," Miss Mudge continued.

"We like walks," the twins said.

"But—did you know you have to pick up their dog doo when you take them out on the walks?" Marguerite asked.

"With your bare hands?" Mack was outraged.

"She's making it up," Teddy reassured him.

"No, not with your bare hands, and no, I'm not making it up. You use a plastic bag or something—like those grocery bags."

The twins looked at her, suspicious, then turned to Quinney. "Will you go with us on the walks?" Mack asked finally.

Quinney laughed. "Sure. Some of the time, anyway."

"Okay, then. We'll take Rags on lots of walks," Mack said.

"With lots and lots of plastic bags for Quinney," Teddy added.

Later, while Brynn was upstairs helping Marguerite pack up the last of her belongings, Quinney and the little boys decided to take the two dogs on a walk around the block. "Take turns holding the leashes," Miss Mudge said. "And mind Quinney."

"We always mind Quinney," Teddy said virtuously, and

they headed off down the dark, empty street, plastic bags flapping.

The boys quickly took the lead, towed behind an eager, inquisitive Rags; Quinney dawdled several paces behind, trying to sort out her feelings.

New dog.

Marguerite leaving.

Baby. No "maybe" about it.

"Hey, Quinney?" a voice behind her said.

Quinney whirled around, heart pounding. It couldn't be—

But it was. "Oh, hi, Cree," she said, cool as she could manage.

"I was just out walking," he said. "I didn't know you had dogs."

"Just one—the sheepdog mix."

"Who's that?" Mack shouted. "Who are you talking to, Quinney?"

"A friend," she called out.

"Nosy little guy," Cree said, laughing.

"You have no idea. He'll be talking about this for days."

"So, what's up? How was the picnic?"

"Still going on," Quinney said. "It's winding down, now."

"Is Marguerite okay?"

"She's going to be fine, I think. I hope."

"Me, too."

They walked along without talking for a while, laughing when Rags jumped at a spooky shadow and soothing hurt feelings when there was a squabble over who was going to hold which dog. "Guess what?" Quinney finally said to Cree. "My mom's going to have another baby." The words didn't sound so—so cataclysmic, Quinney thought, when she said them aloud. They sounded almost normal.

"Oh, cool," Cree said.

Quinney smiled. "It is cool, I guess," she said.

They walked some more. "I like your hair, by the way," Cree said.

"Quinney," Teddy shrieked. "Quick, get a bag—he's doing something!"

"And so Cree was the one who cleaned it up. Teddy told him he was brave," Quinney reported to Marguerite an hour later. Cross-legged on the kitchen floor, she nestled the kitchen phone against her shoulder and reached out to sweep some stray kibble chunks into a tidy little pile.

"How romantic," Marguerite teased. "And you just happened to bump into him! You can tell your children some day. I'm just glad you were wearing a little makeup."

"Marguerite!"

"Oh, don't bust a gut," Marguerite laughed.

"I can't believe I was going to tell you that I miss you," Quinney said, laughing, too.

"Oh, right," Marguerite scoffed. "You miss all the dirty

clothes on the floor. You miss the snarly brown hair in your hairbrush. You miss the noise from my Walkman while you're trying to do your homework or go to sleep, is that it?"

"Well, when you put it *that* way . . ."

"You are just pathetic," Marguerite teased.

"I guess."

Lying in bed that night, Quinney gazed around her moon-lit room.

Spotless.

She thought of getting up, trotting over to her closet, and reaching into the hamper, emerging with an armful of dirty clothes. She could scatter them across the bedroom floor for old times' sake: a sweatshirt here, a faded night-gown there.

No, she thought, smiling. She might be a little bit looser, but she hadn't changed all that much. It was nice having her orderly room all to herself again.

Things had changed, though, she thought. Monty was gone, and the twins were no longer the indivisible unit they'd once been.

And in spite of tonight, Brynnie and Marguerite prob-ably wouldn't be seeing as much of each other. Quinney might not even be seeing as much of Brynn, if Brynnie and Charlotte became really good friends.

But I'm making new friends, too, Quinney reassured herself, thinking of Miss Mudge and Rags and Cree—and of her new relationship with Marguerite, for that matter.

"Good-bye, Monty," Quinney said aloud in the dark. "It was nice knowing you. And good-bye Teddy-Mack, and Quinney-Brynnie-Marguerite."

She thought for a moment.

"Hello, Quinney."